01/19

REBEL'S REPORT

ROGUE ONE: VOLUME 1

MISSION:
Find and extract Jyn Erso

ALIAS "LIANA HALLIK"

NOTES:
Daughter of Galen Erso (known Imperial research scientist). Goes by the alias "Liana Hallik." Known associate of rebel extremist Saw Gerrera.

SAW GERRERA

GALEN ERSO

STATUS:
Rebel intelligence officers to be dispatched to retrieve target.

CAPTAIN CASIAN ANDOR

K-2SO

CREDITS:

WRITER • Jody Houser
ARTISTS • Emilio Laiso & Oscar Bazaldua
COLORIST • Rachelle Rosenberg
LETTERER • VC's Clayton Cowles
COVER ARTIST • Phil Noto
PRODUCTION DESIGN • Carlos Lao
EDITOR • Heather Antos
SUPERVISING EDITOR • Jordan D. White
EXECUTIVE EDITOR • C.B. Cebulski
EDITOR IN CHIEF • Axel Alonso
CHIEF CREATIVE OFFICER • Joe Quesada
PRESIDENT • Dan Buckley
EXECUTIVE PRODUCER • Alan Fine

Based on the screenplay
by Chris Weitz and Tony Gilroy

Based on a story by
John Knoll and Gary Whitta

LUCASFILM:

SENIOR EDITOR • Frank Parisi
CREATIVE DIRECTOR • Michael Siglain
LUCASFILM STORY GROUP • James Waugh, Leland Chee, Matt Martin, Rayne Roberts

marvelkids.com

ABDO Spotlight

ABDOPUBLISHING.COM

Reinforced library bound edition published in 2019 by Spotlight,
a division of ABDO, PO Box 398166, Minneapolis, Minnesota 55439.
Spotlight produces high-quality reinforced library bound editions for
schools and libraries. Published by agreement with Marvel Characters, Inc.

Printed in the United States of America, North Mankato, Minnesota.
042018
092018

THIS BOOK CONTAINS
RECYCLED MATERIALS

marvelkids.com

Library of Congress Control Number: 2017961400

Publisher's Cataloging in Publication Data

Names: Houser, Jody, author. | Laiso, Emilio; Bazaldua, Oscar; Rosenberg, Rachelle; Villanelli, Paolo, illustrators.
Title: Rogue One / writer: Jody Houser; art: Emilio Laiso, Oscar Bazaldua, Rachelle Rosenberg, and Paolo Villanelli.
Description: Reinforced library bound edition. | Minneapolis, MN : Spotlight, 2019 | Series: Star Wars: Rogue One | Volume 1 written by Jody Houser; illustrated by Emilio Laiso, Oscar Bazaldua and Rachelle Rosenberg. | Volumes 2, 4, 5, and 6 written by Jody Houser; illustrated by Emilio Laiso and Rachelle Rosenberg. | Volume 3 written by Jody Houser; illustrated by Paolo Villanelli and Rachelle Rosenberg.
Summary: Scientist Galen Erso is taken from his home and forced to work on the Empire's secret planet-killing weapon, leaving his daughter, Jyn, to grow up on her own. Fifteen years later, Galen leaks information on the weapon, through a message he sends to some bandits on the moon Jedha. Now, the rebels of the Alliance want to know if the rumors of an Imperial Death Star are true. They'll need Jyn to help retrieve the message and, possibly, find her father.
Identifiers: ISBN 9781532141683 (Volume 1) | ISBN 9781532141690 (Volume 2) | ISBN 9781532141706 (Volume 3) | ISBN 9781532141713 (Volume 4) | ISBN 9781532141720 (Volume 5) | ISBN 9781532141737 (Volume 6)
Subjects: LCSH: Star Wars films--Juvenile fiction. | Weapons--Juvenile fiction. | Space colonies--Juvenile fiction. | Imaginary wars and battles--Juvenile fiction. | Comic books, strips, etc.--Juvenile fiction.
Classification: DDC 741.5--dc23

ABDO

Spotlight

A Division of ABDO
abdopublishing.com

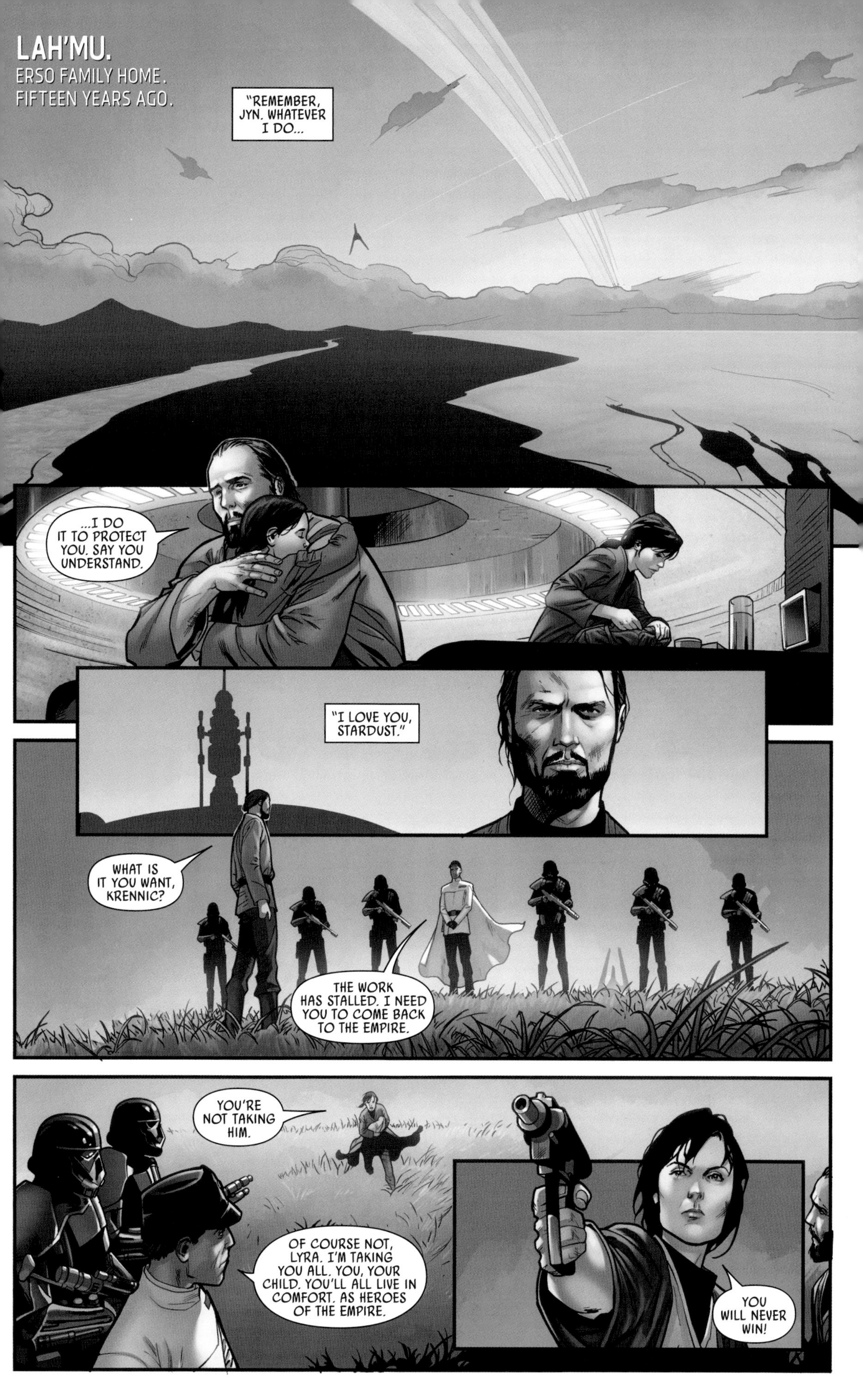
LAH'MU.
ERSO FAMILY HOME. FIFTEEN YEARS AGO.
"REMEMBER, JYN. WHATEVER I DO...
...I DO IT TO PROTECT YOU. SAY YOU UNDERSTAND.
"I LOVE YOU, STARDUST."
WHAT IS IT YOU WANT, KRENNIC?
THE WORK HAS STALLED. I NEED YOU TO COME BACK TO THE EMPIRE.
YOU'RE NOT TAKING HIM.
OF COURSE NOT, LYRA. I'M TAKING YOU ALL. YOU, YOUR CHILD. YOU'LL ALL LIVE IN COMFORT. AS HEROES OF THE EMPIRE.
YOU WILL NEVER WIN!

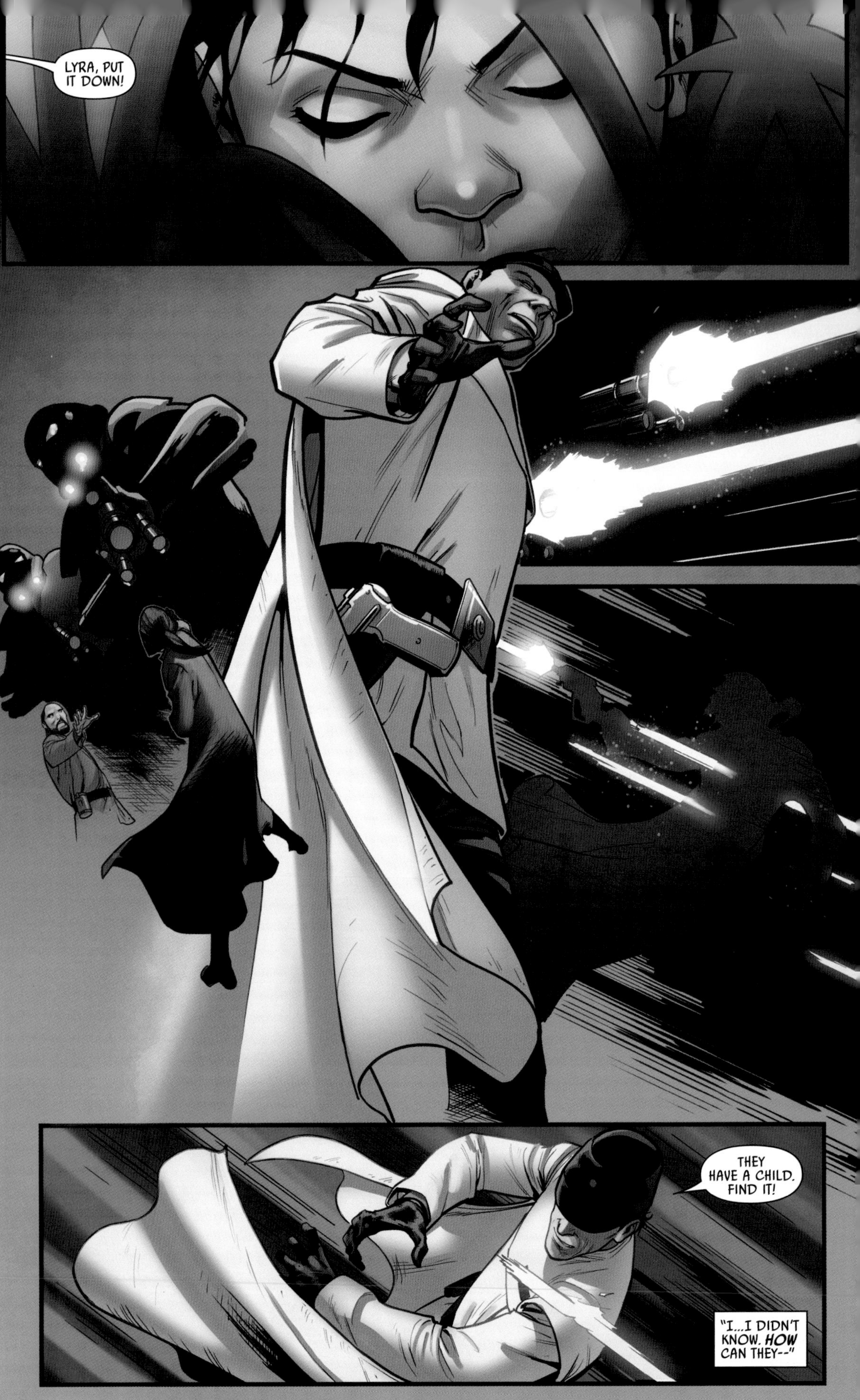
LYRA, PUT IT DOWN!
THEY HAVE A CHILD. FIND IT!
"I...I DIDN'T KNOW. HOW CAN THEY--"

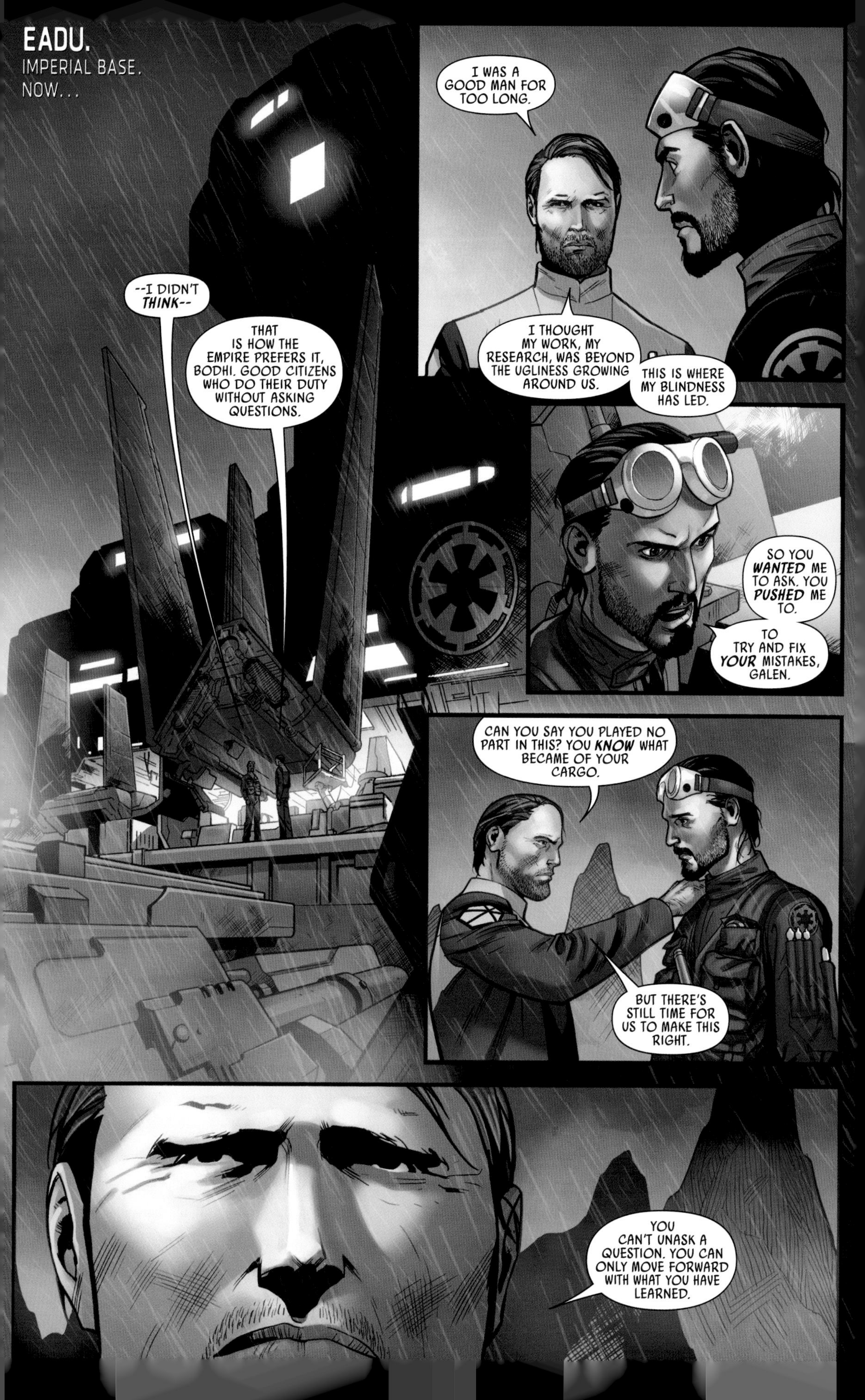
EADU.
IMPERIAL BASE.
NOW...
I WAS A GOOD MAN FOR TOO LONG.
--I DIDN'T THINK--
THAT IS HOW THE EMPIRE PREFERS IT, BODHI. GOOD CITIZENS WHO DO THEIR DUTY WITHOUT ASKING QUESTIONS.
I THOUGHT MY WORK, MY RESEARCH, WAS BEYOND THE UGLINESS GROWING AROUND US.
THIS IS WHERE MY BLINDNESS HAS LED.
SO YOU WANTED ME TO ASK. YOU PUSHED ME TO.
TO TRY AND FIX YOUR MISTAKES, GALEN.
CAN YOU SAY YOU PLAYED NO PART IN THIS? YOU KNOW WHAT BECAME OF YOUR CARGO.
BUT THERE'S STILL TIME FOR US TO MAKE THIS RIGHT.
YOU CAN'T UNASK A QUESTION. YOU CAN ONLY MOVE FORWARD WITH WHAT YOU HAVE LEARNED.

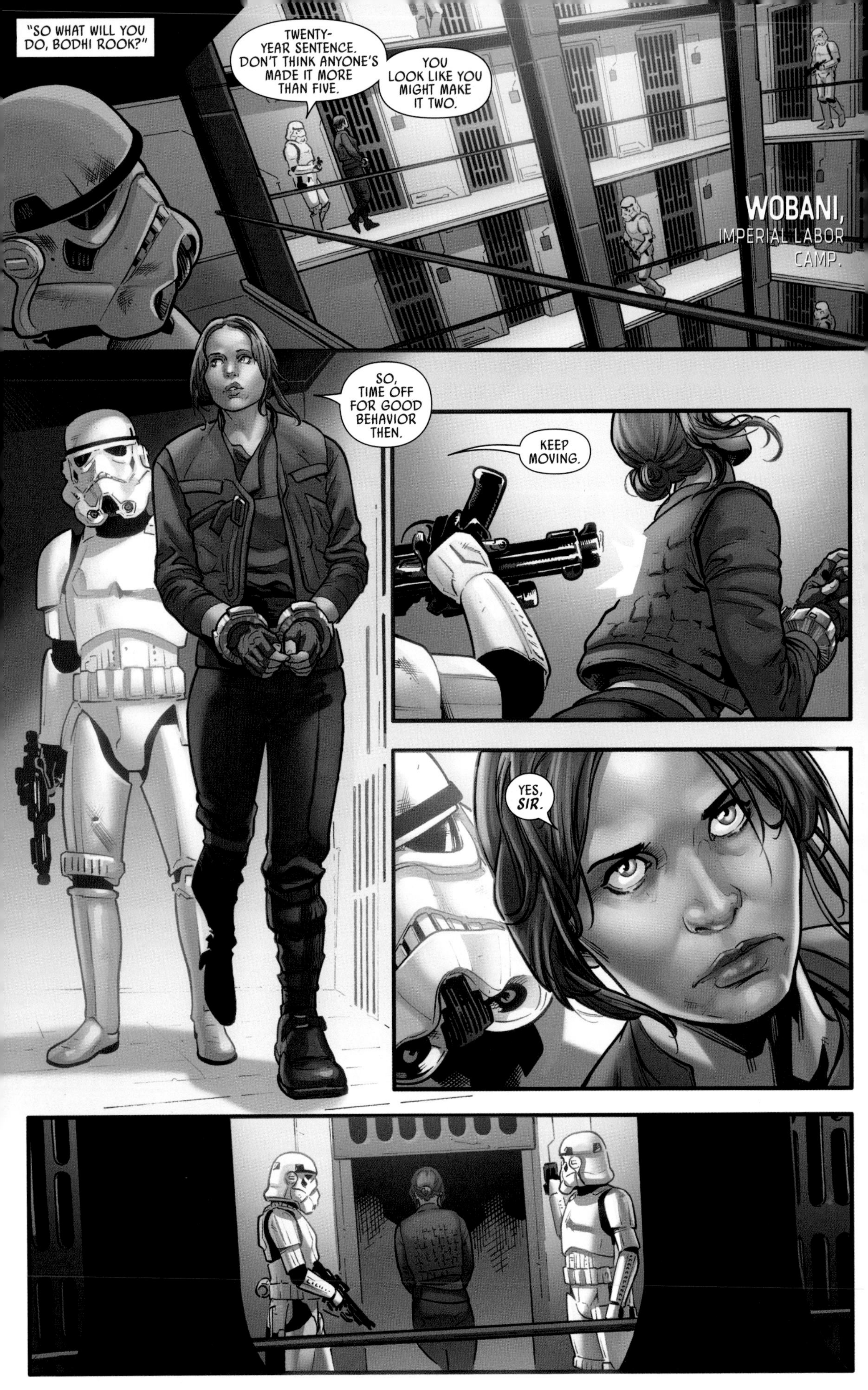
"SO WHAT WILL YOU DO, BODHI ROOK?"
TWENTY-YEAR SENTENCE. DON'T THINK ANYONE'S MADE IT MORE THAN FIVE.
YOU LOOK LIKE YOU MIGHT MAKE IT TWO.
WOBANI, IMPERIAL LABOR CAMP.
SO, TIME OFF FOR GOOD BEHAVIOR THEN.
KEEP MOVING.
YES, *SIR*.

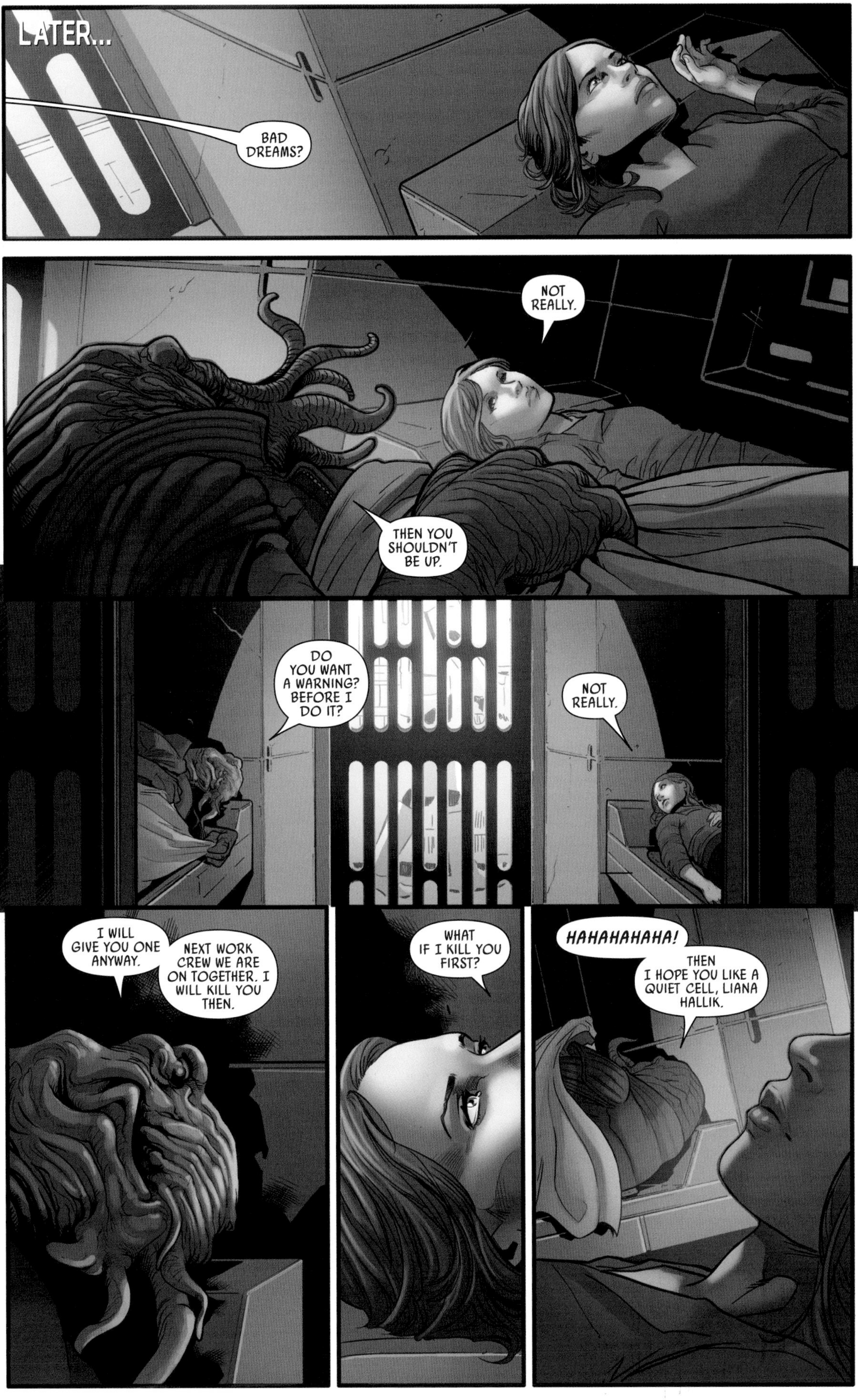
LATER...
BAD DREAMS?
NOT REALLY.
THEN YOU SHOULDN'T BE UP.
DO YOU WANT A WARNING? BEFORE I DO IT?
NOT REALLY.
I WILL GIVE YOU ONE ANYWAY.
NEXT WORK CREW WE ARE ON TOGETHER, I WILL KILL YOU THEN.
WHAT IF I KILL YOU FIRST?
HAHAHAHAHA!
THEN I HOPE YOU LIKE A QUIET CELL, LIANA HALLIK.

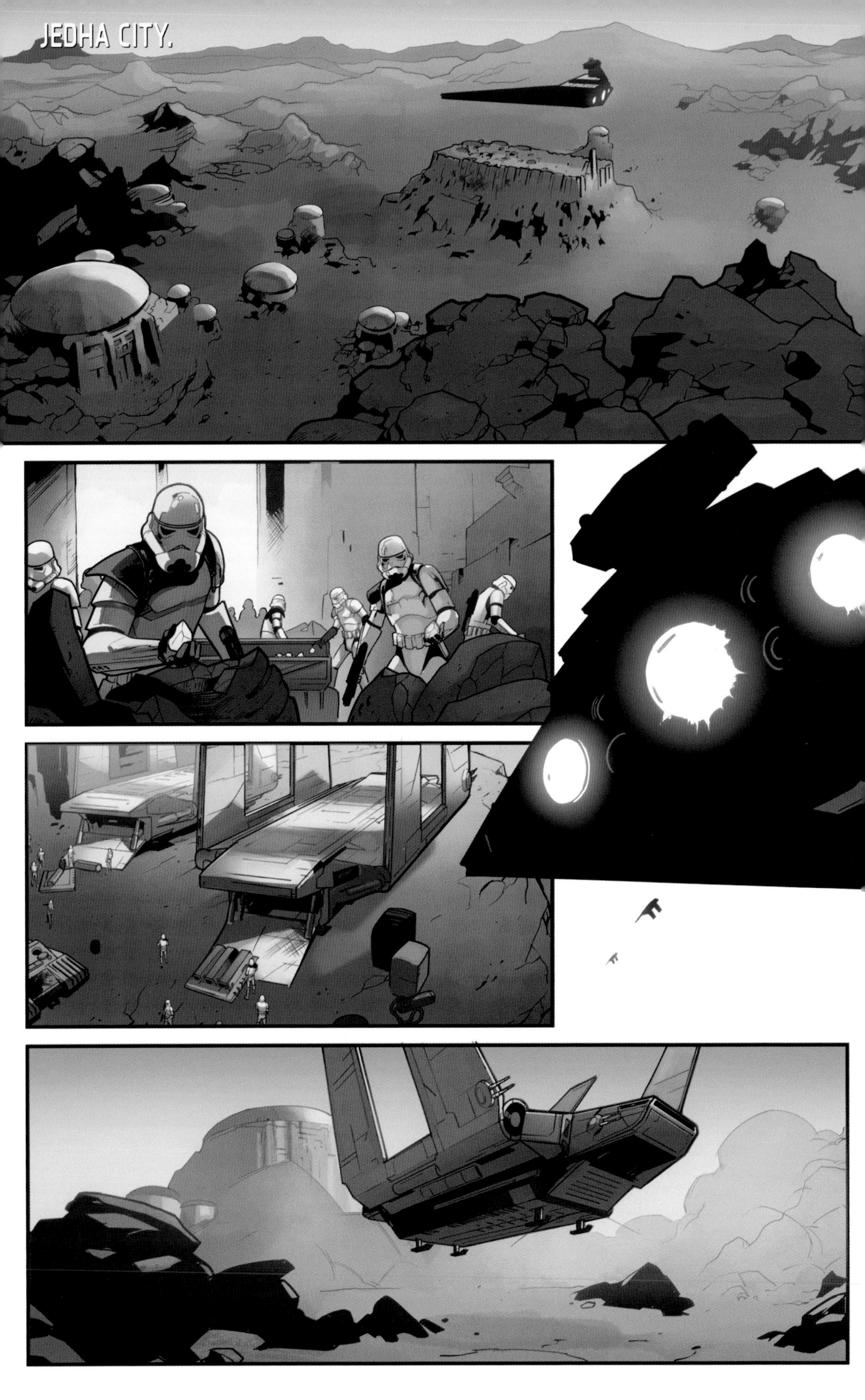
JEDHA CITY.

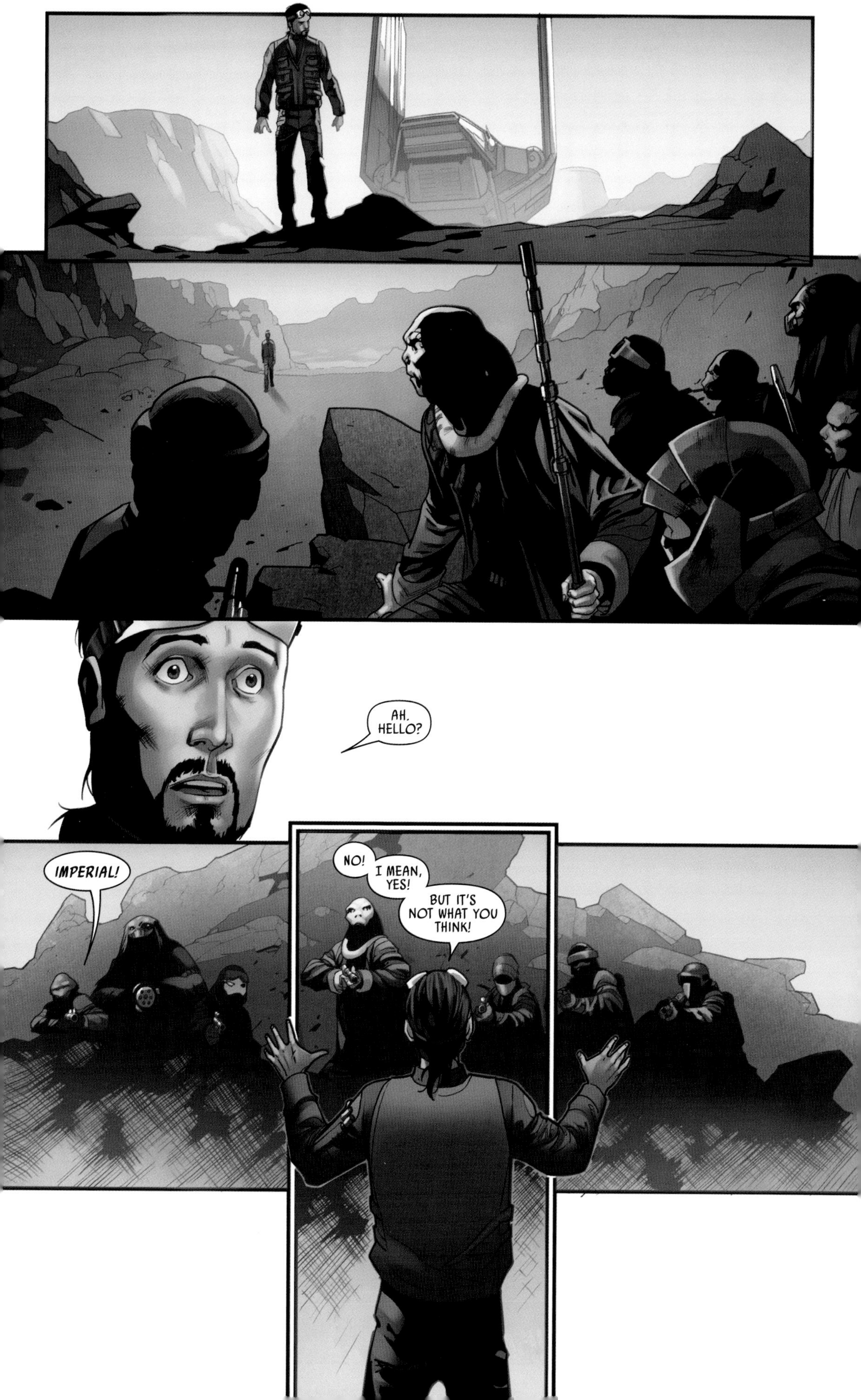
AH. HELLO?
IMPERIAL!
NO!
I MEAN, YES!
BUT IT'S NOT WHAT YOU THINK!

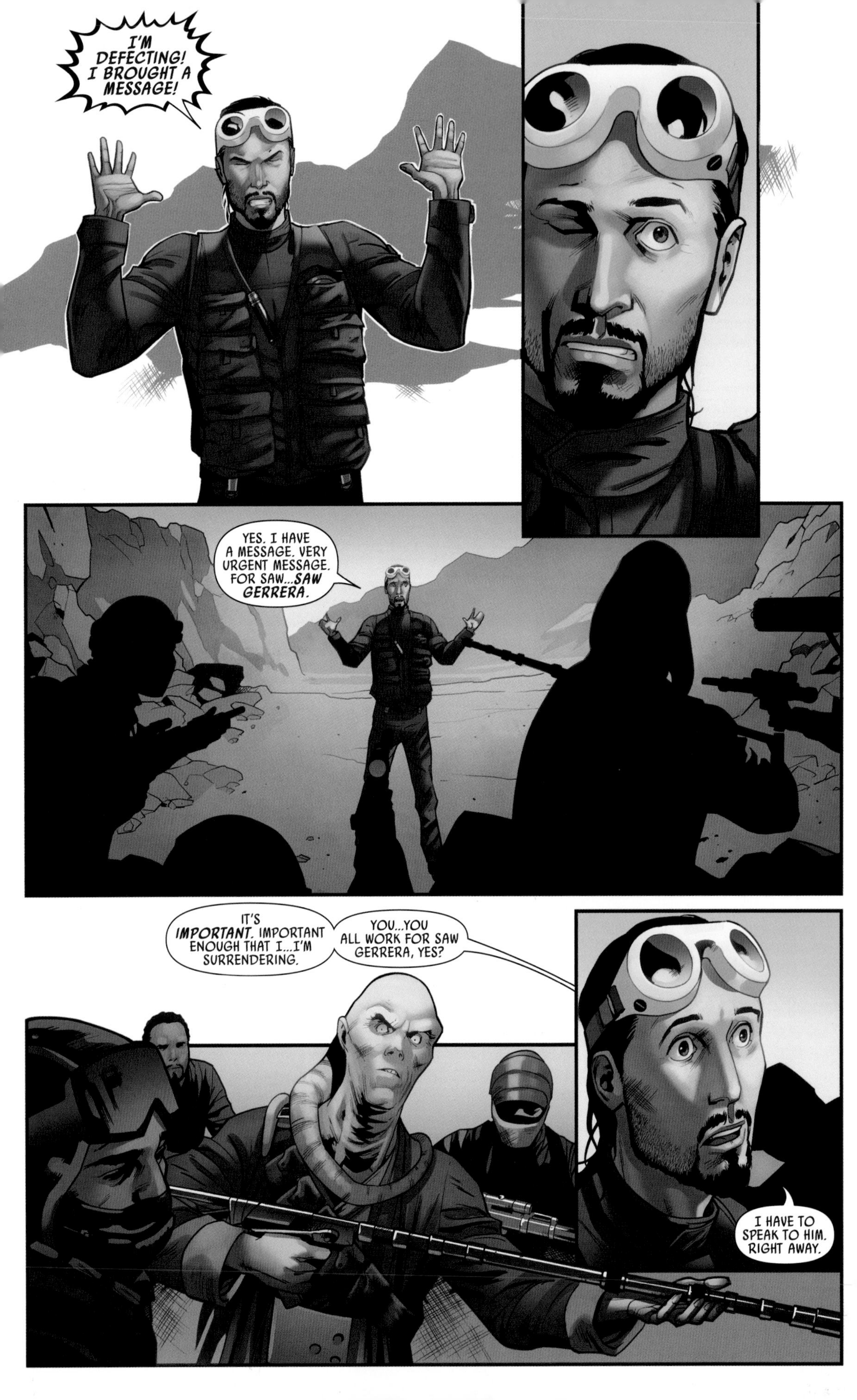
I'M DEFECTING! I BROUGHT A MESSAGE!
YES. I HAVE A MESSAGE. VERY URGENT MESSAGE. FOR SAW...SAW GERRERA.
IT'S IMPORTANT. IMPORTANT ENOUGH THAT I...I'M SURRENDERING.
YOU...YOU ALL WORK FOR SAW GERRERA, YES?
I HAVE TO SPEAK TO HIM. RIGHT AWAY.

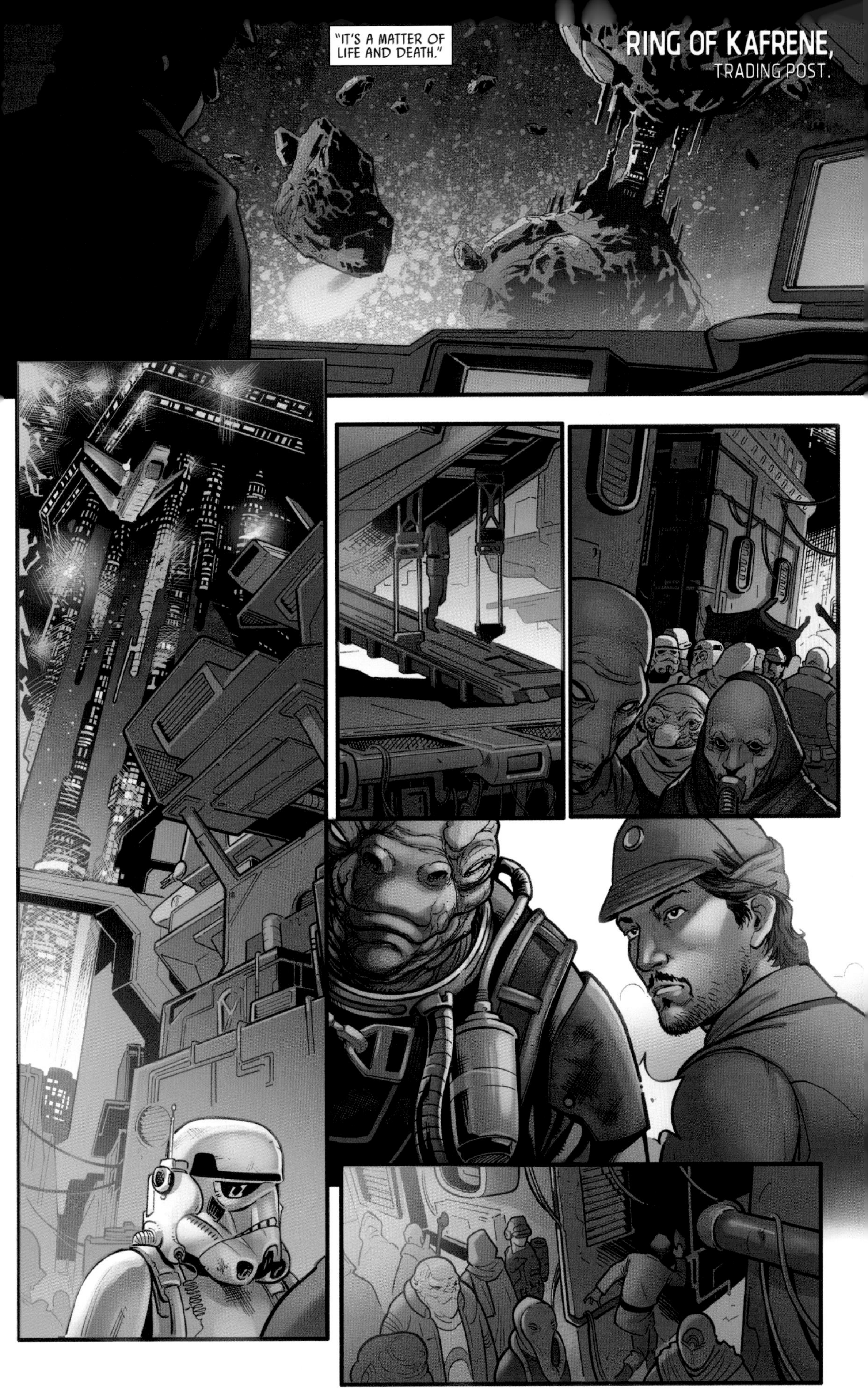
"IT'S A MATTER OF LIFE AND DEATH."
RING OF KAFRENE,
TRADING POST.

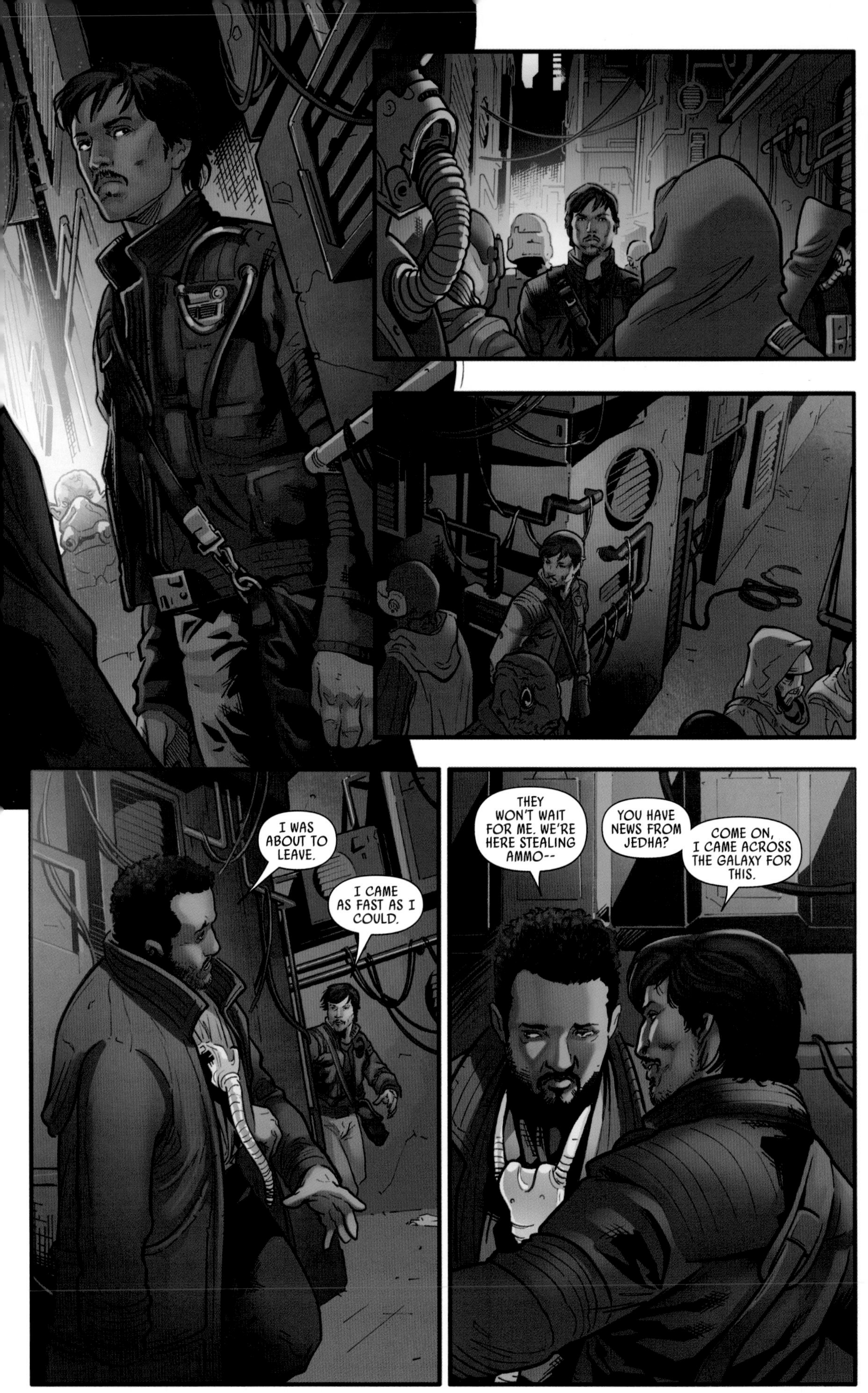
I WAS ABOUT TO LEAVE.
I CAME AS FAST AS I COULD.
THEY WON'T WAIT FOR ME. WE'RE HERE STEALING AMMO--
YOU HAVE NEWS FROM JEDHA?
COME ON, I CAME ACROSS THE GALAXY FOR THIS.

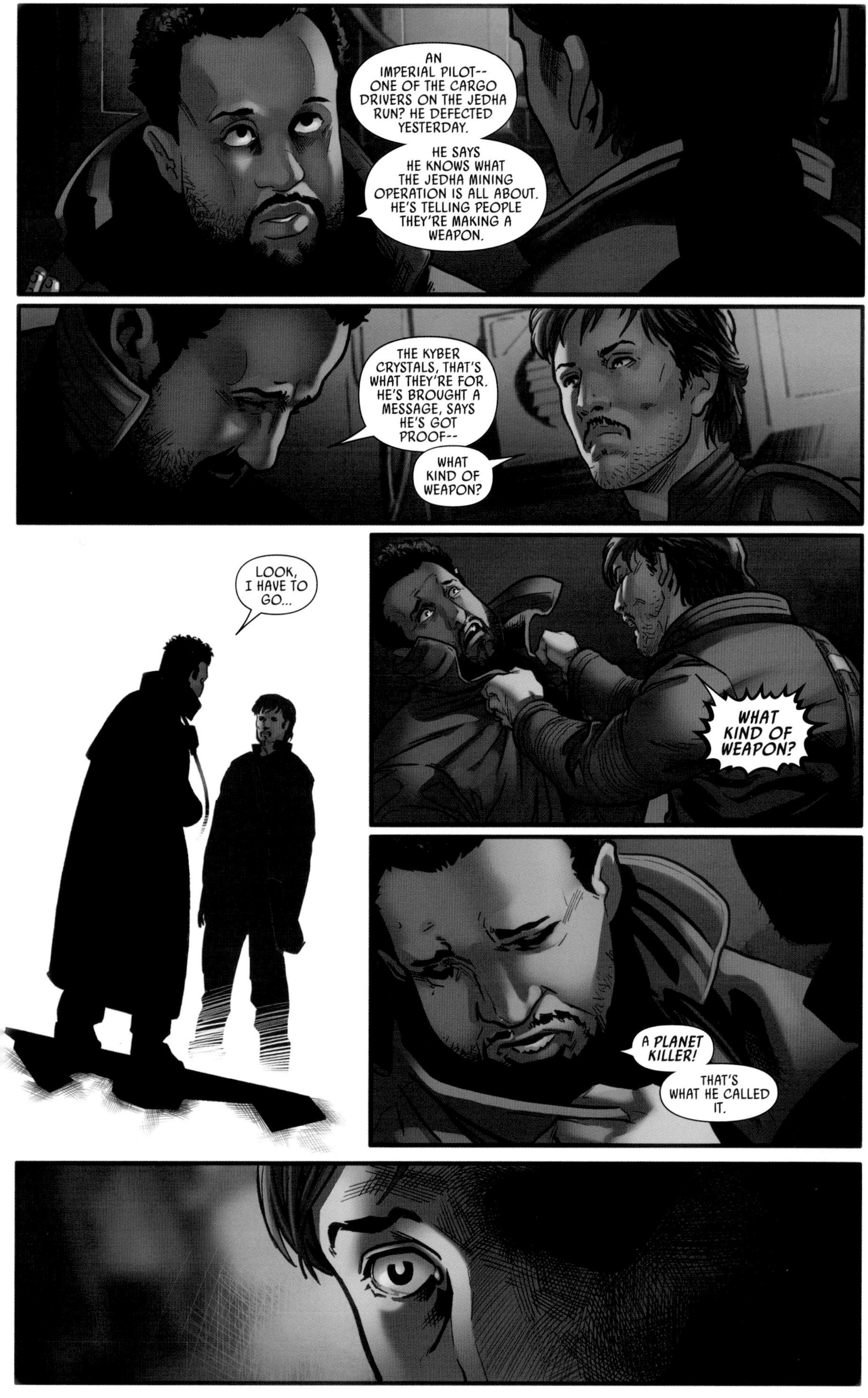
AN IMPERIAL PILOT-- ONE OF THE CARGO DRIVERS ON THE JEDHA RUN? HE DEFECTED YESTERDAY.
HE SAYS HE KNOWS WHAT THE JEDHA MINING OPERATION IS ALL ABOUT. HE'S TELLING PEOPLE THEY'RE MAKING A WEAPON.
THE KYBER CRYSTALS, THAT'S WHAT THEY'RE FOR. HE'S BROUGHT A MESSAGE, SAYS HE'S GOT PROOF--
WHAT KIND OF WEAPON?
LOOK, I HAVE TO GO...
WHAT KIND OF WEAPON?
A PLANET KILLER!
THAT'S WHAT HE CALLED IT.

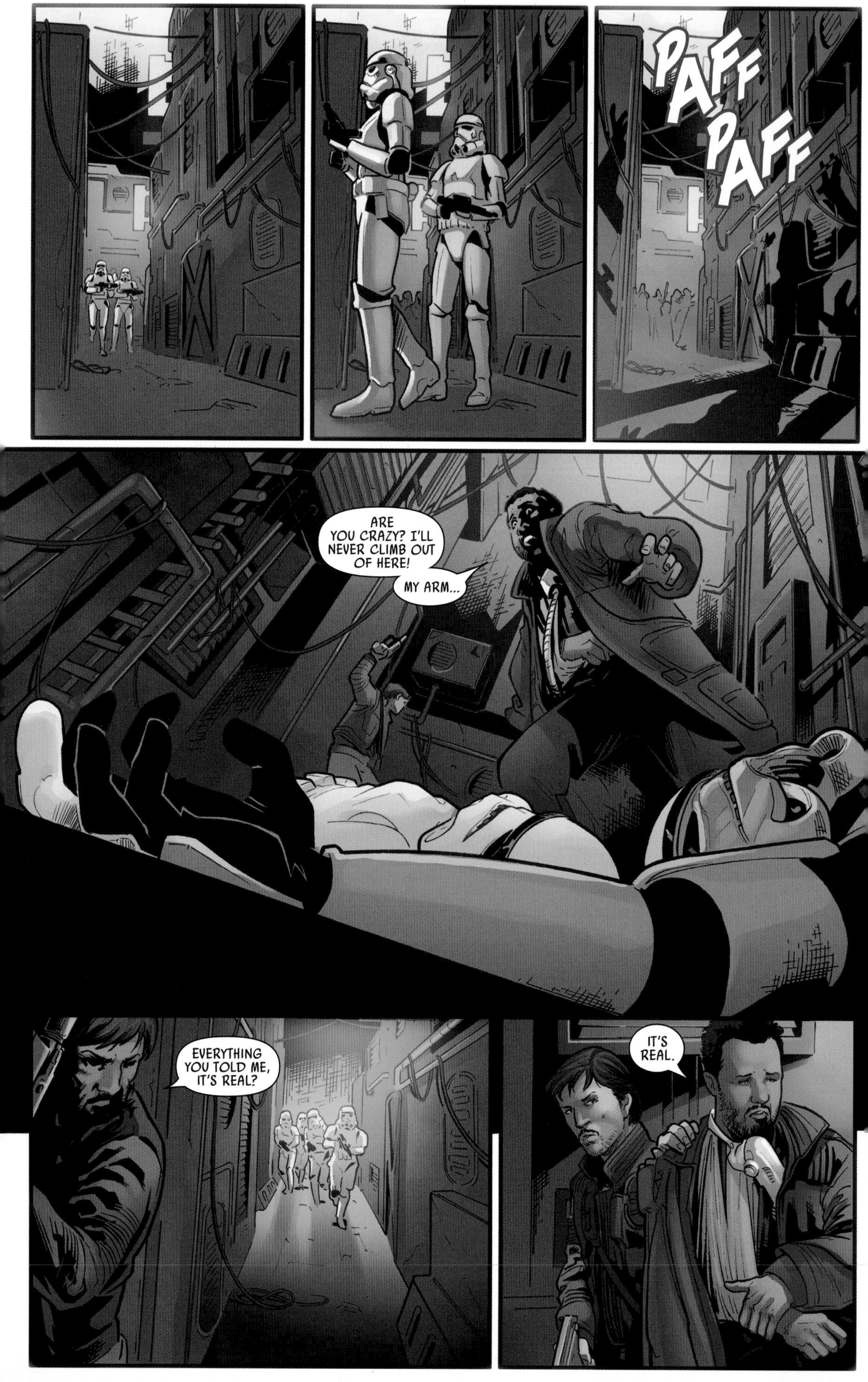
PAFF PAFF
ARE YOU CRAZY? I'LL NEVER CLIMB OUT OF HERE!
MY ARM...
EVERYTHING YOU TOLD ME, IT'S REAL?
IT'S REAL.

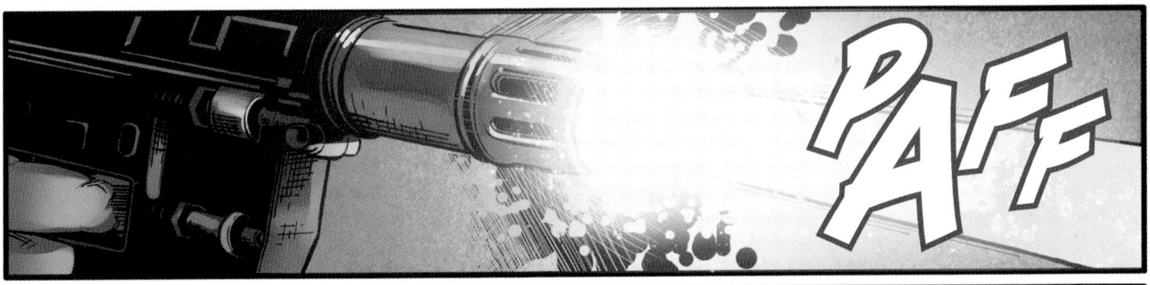
PAFF

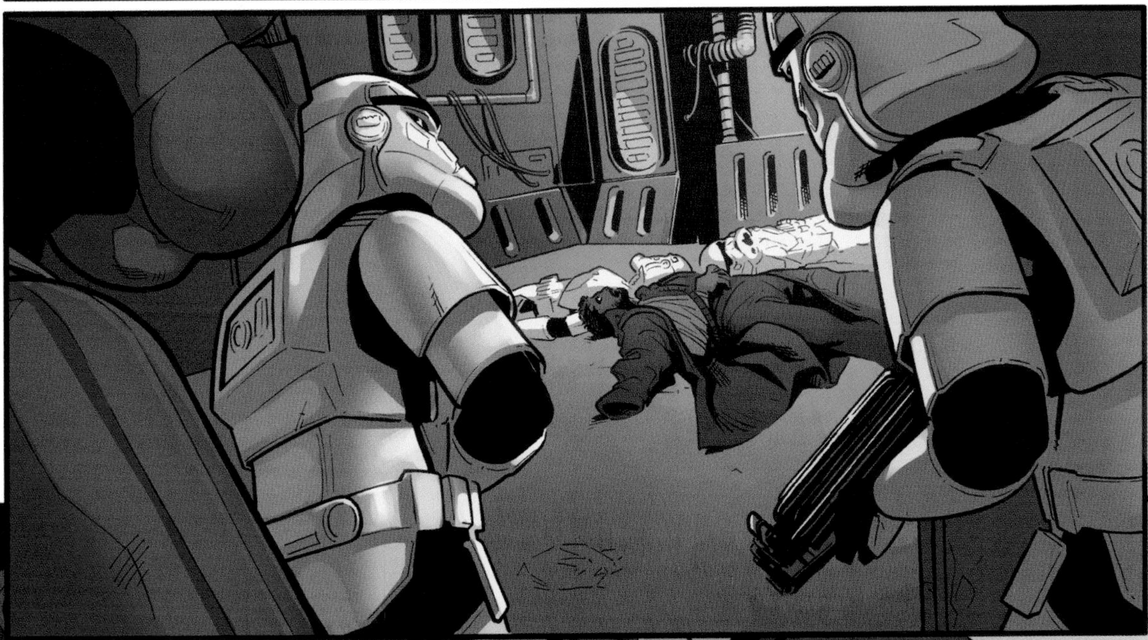

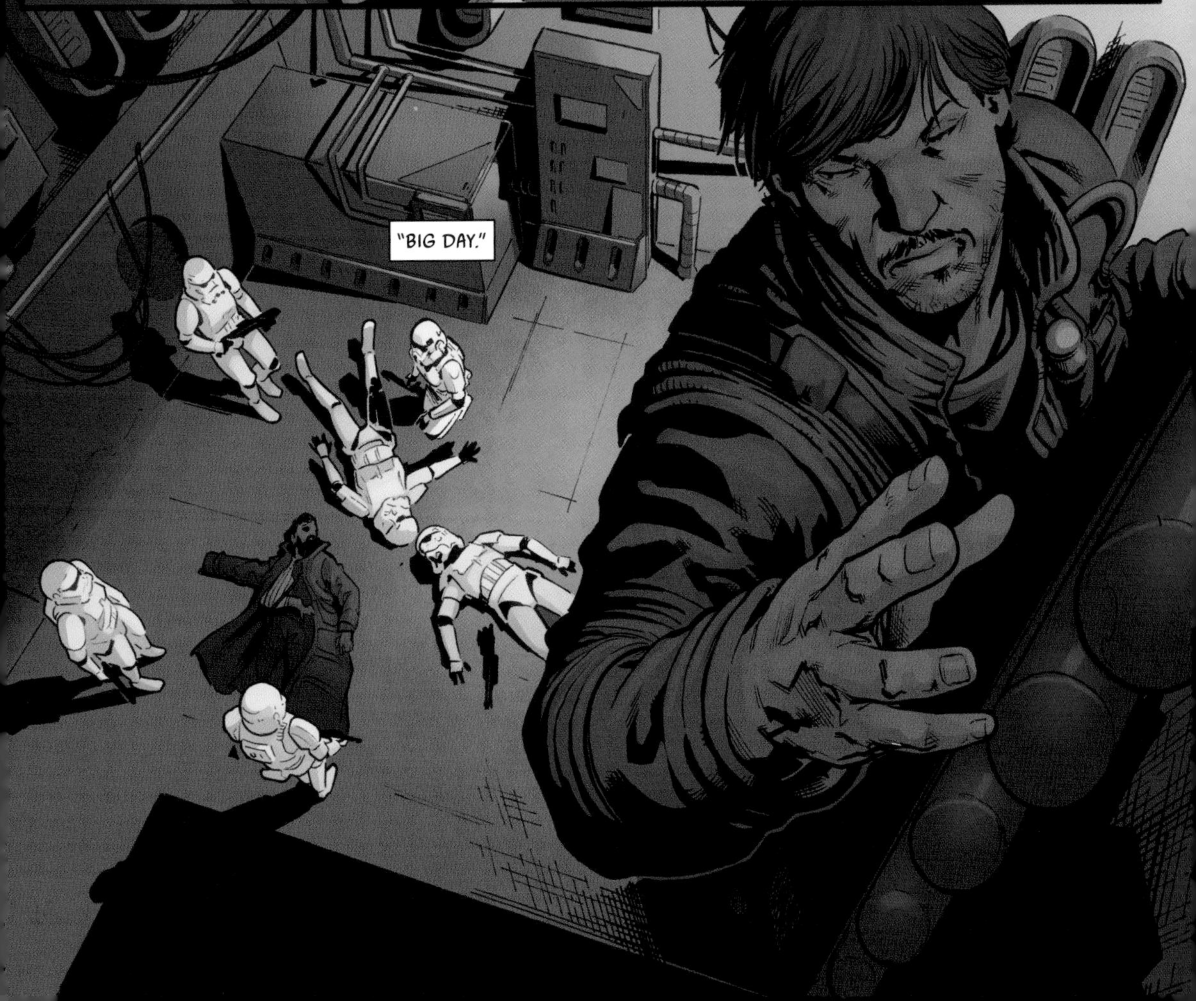
"BIG DAY."

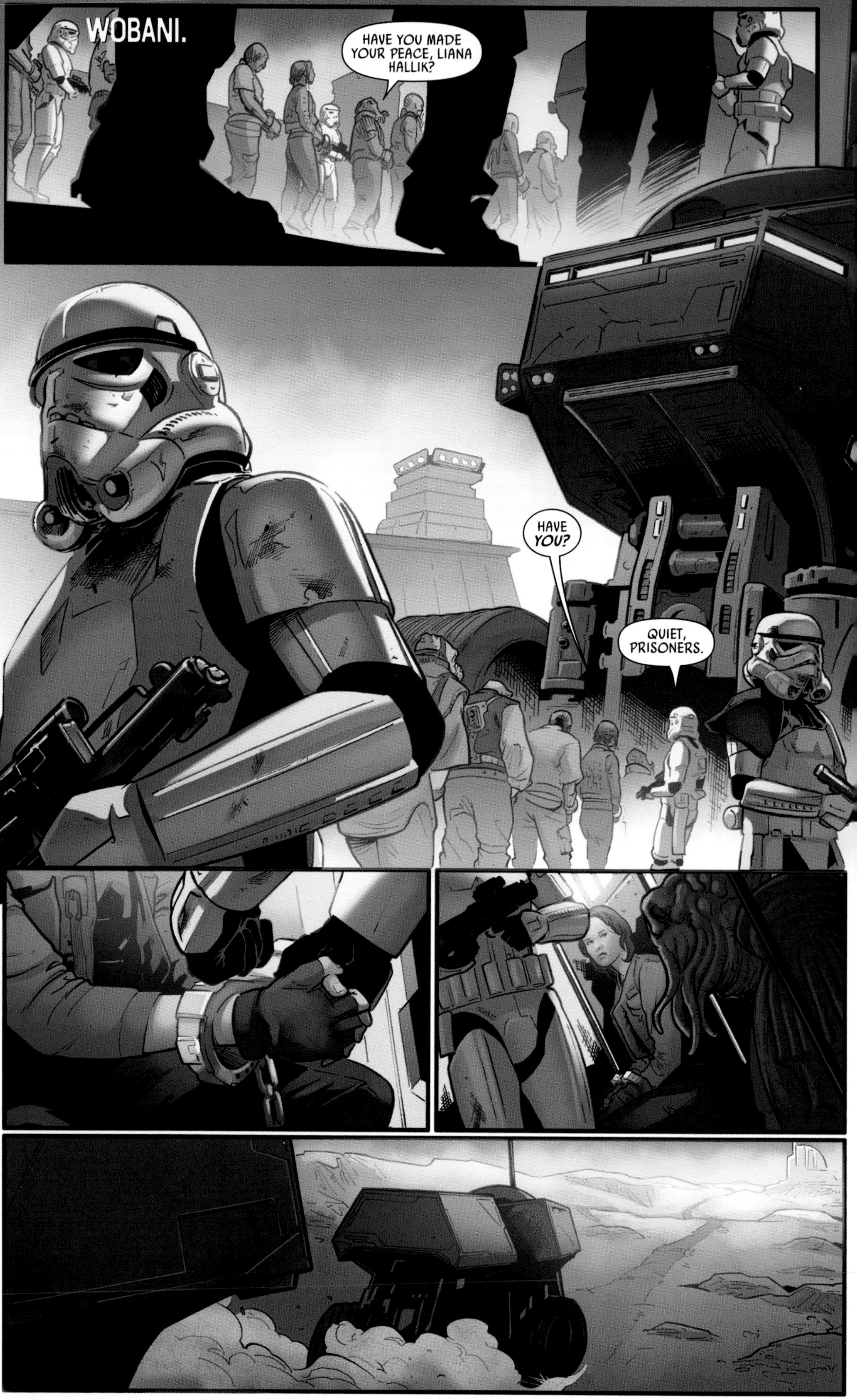
WOBANI.
HAVE YOU MADE YOUR PEACE, LIANA HALLIK?
HAVE *YOU?*
QUIET, PRISONERS.

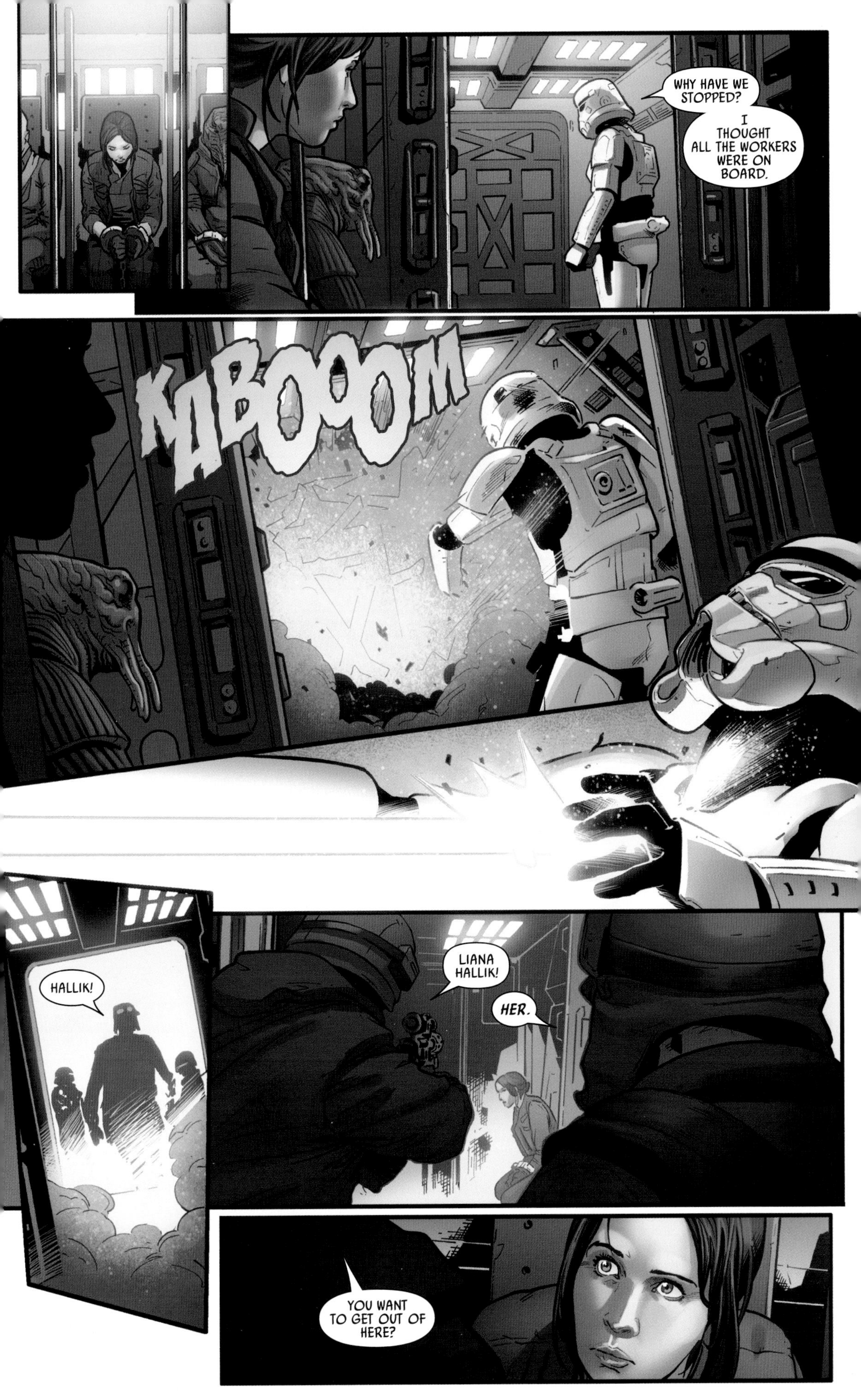
WHY HAVE WE STOPPED?
I THOUGHT ALL THE WORKERS WERE ON BOARD.
KABOOOM
HALLIK!
LIANA HALLIK!
HER.
YOU WANT TO GET OUT OF HERE?

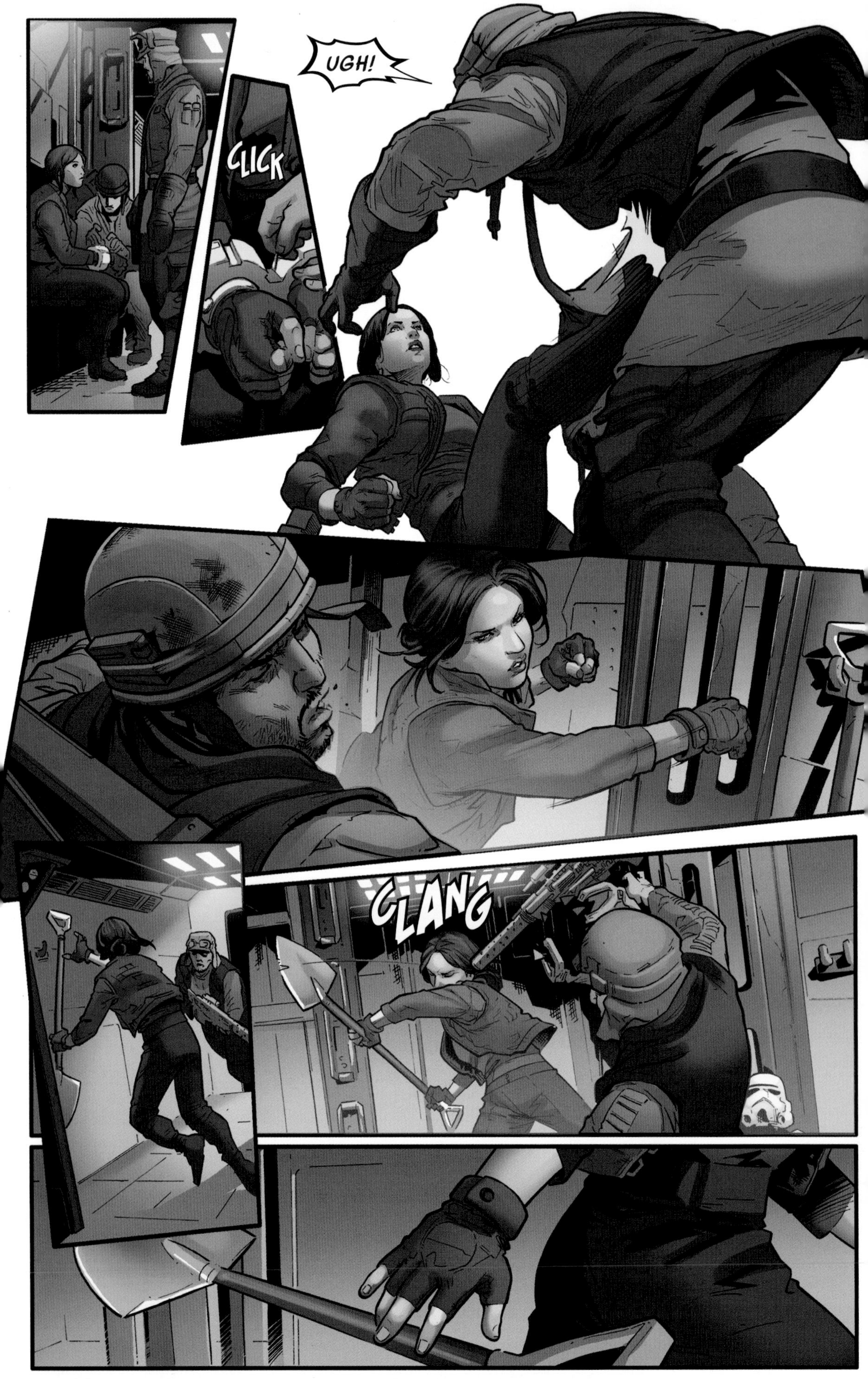
CLICK
UGH!
CLANG

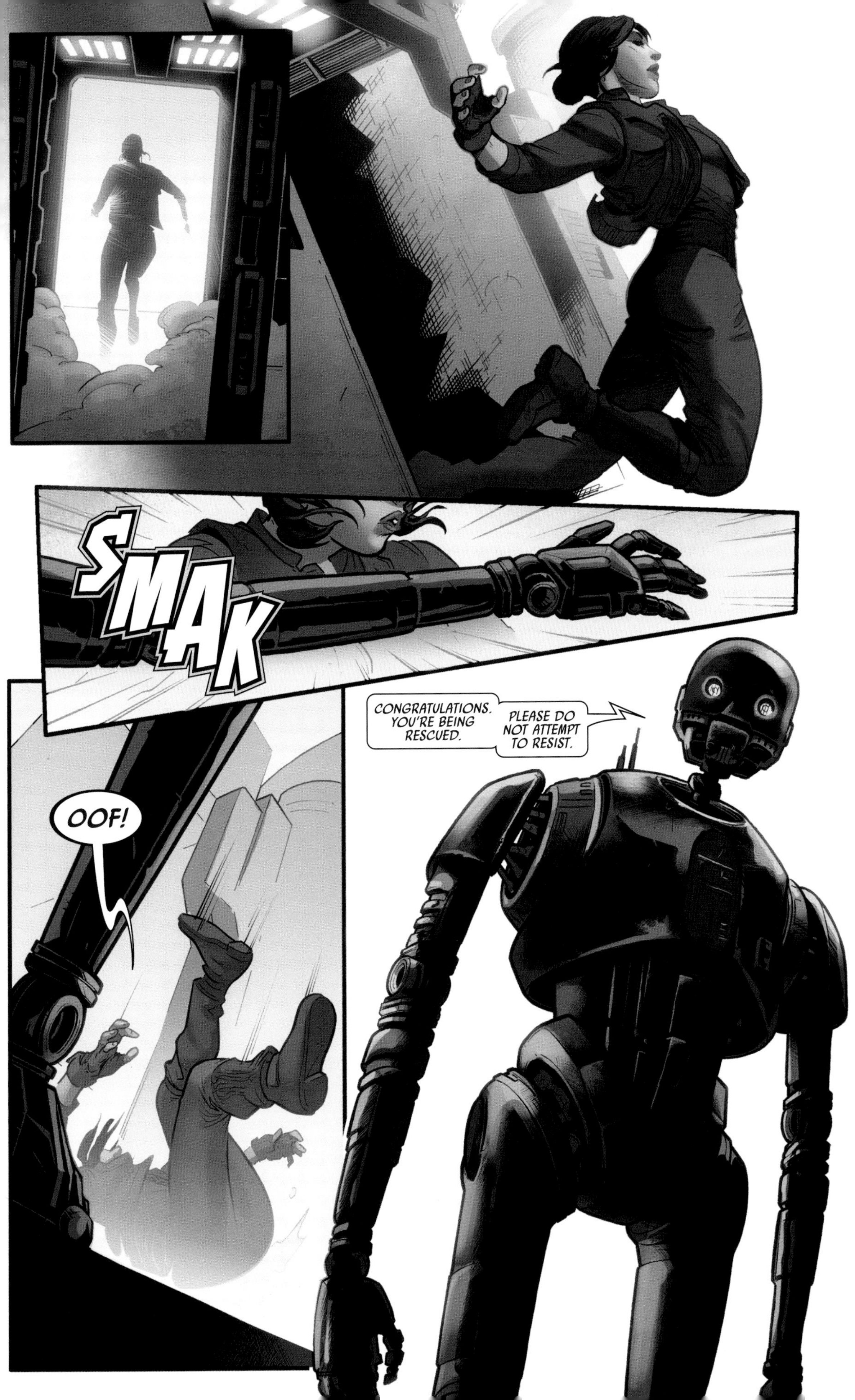
SMAK
CONGRATULATIONS. YOU'RE BEING RESCUED.
PLEASE DO NOT ATTEMPT TO RESIST.
OOF!

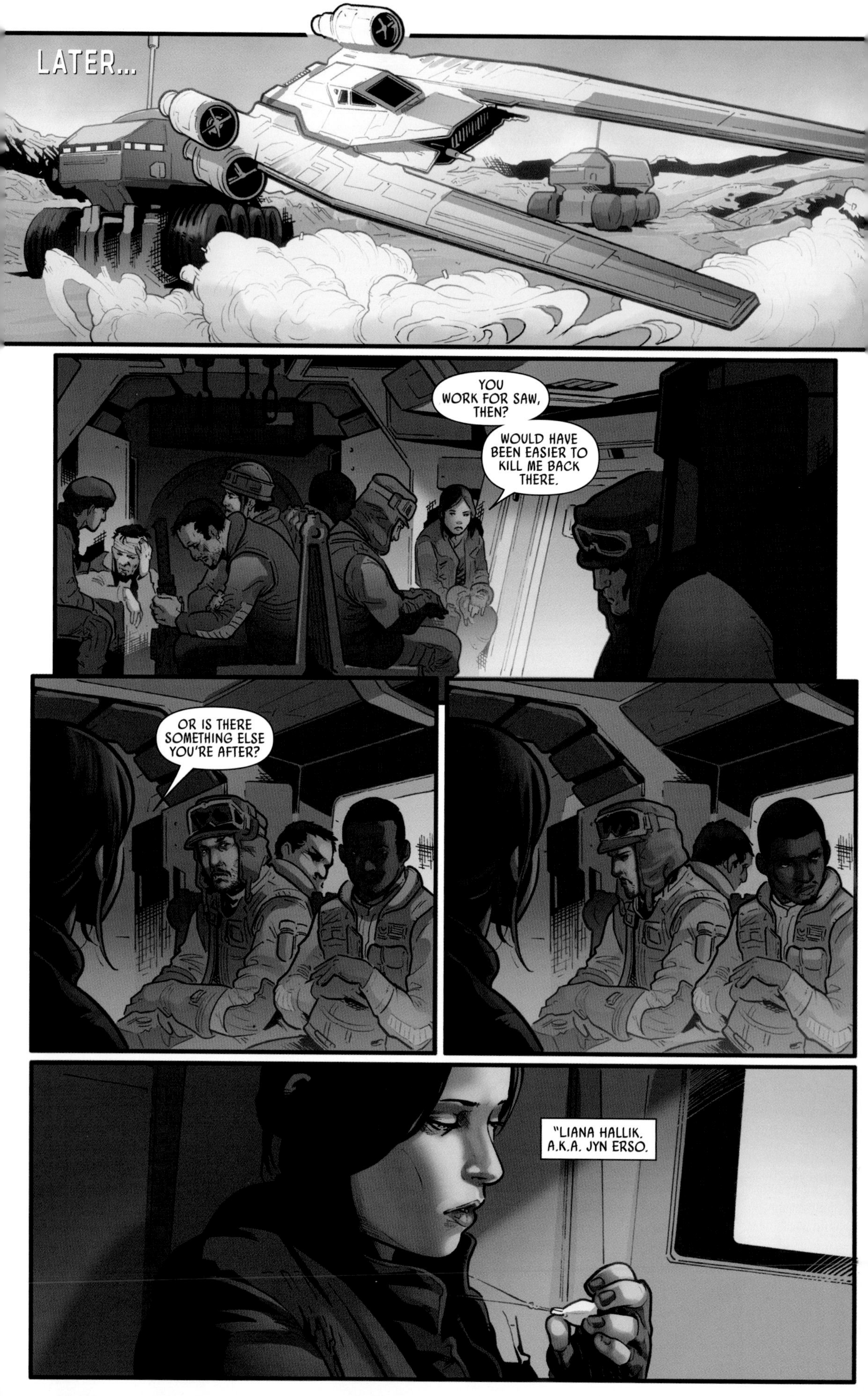
LATER...
YOU WORK FOR SAW, THEN?
WOULD HAVE BEEN EASIER TO KILL ME BACK THERE.
OR IS THERE SOMETHING ELSE YOU'RE AFTER?
"LIANA HALLIK. A.K.A. JYN ERSO.

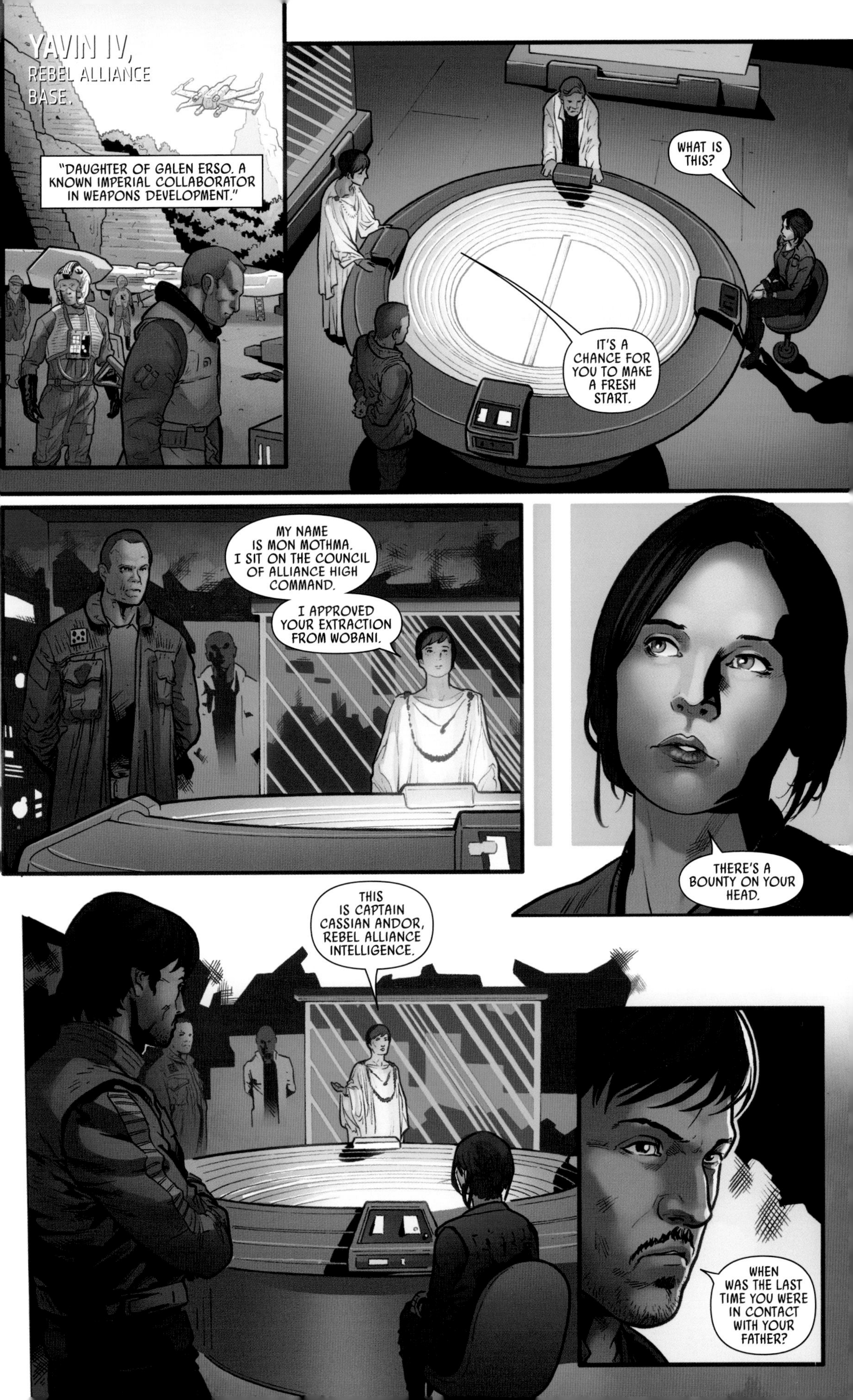
YAVIN IV,
REBEL ALLIANCE BASE.
"DAUGHTER OF GALEN ERSO. A KNOWN IMPERIAL COLLABORATOR IN WEAPONS DEVELOPMENT."
WHAT IS THIS?
IT'S A CHANCE FOR YOU TO MAKE A FRESH START.
MY NAME IS MON MOTHMA. I SIT ON THE COUNCIL OF ALLIANCE HIGH COMMAND.
I APPROVED YOUR EXTRACTION FROM WOBANI.
THERE'S A BOUNTY ON YOUR HEAD.
THIS IS CAPTAIN CASSIAN ANDOR, REBEL ALLIANCE INTELLIGENCE.
WHEN WAS THE LAST TIME YOU WERE IN CONTACT WITH YOUR FATHER?

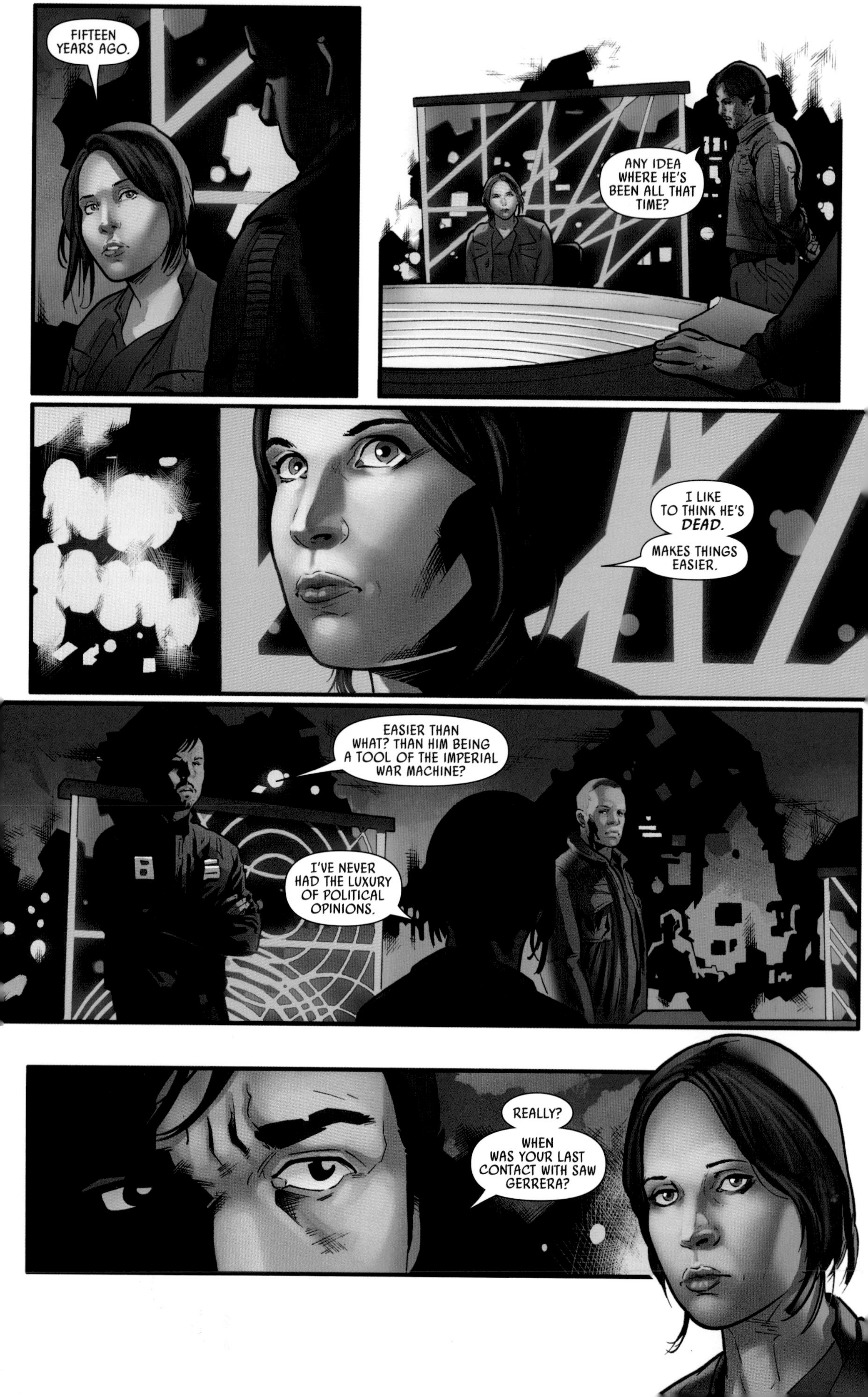
FIFTEEN YEARS AGO.
ANY IDEA WHERE HE'S BEEN ALL THAT TIME?
I LIKE TO THINK HE'S *DEAD.*
MAKES THINGS EASIER.
EASIER THAN WHAT? THAN HIM BEING A TOOL OF THE IMPERIAL WAR MACHINE?
I'VE NEVER HAD THE LUXURY OF POLITICAL OPINIONS.
REALLY?
WHEN WAS YOUR LAST CONTACT WITH SAW GERRERA?

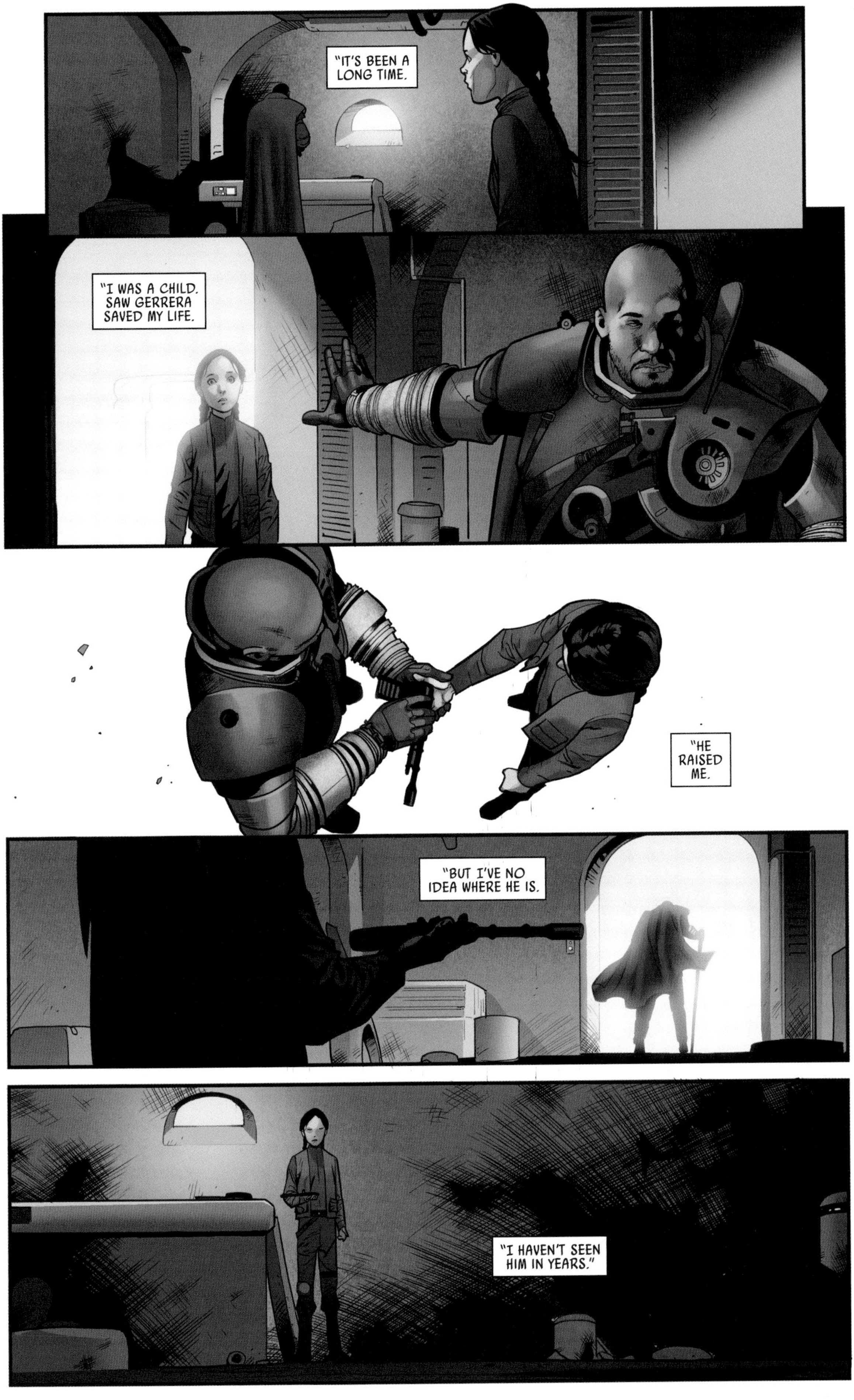
"IT'S BEEN A LONG TIME.
"I WAS A CHILD. SAW GERRERA SAVED MY LIFE.
"HE RAISED ME.
"BUT I'VE NO IDEA WHERE HE IS.
"I HAVEN'T SEEN HIM IN YEARS."

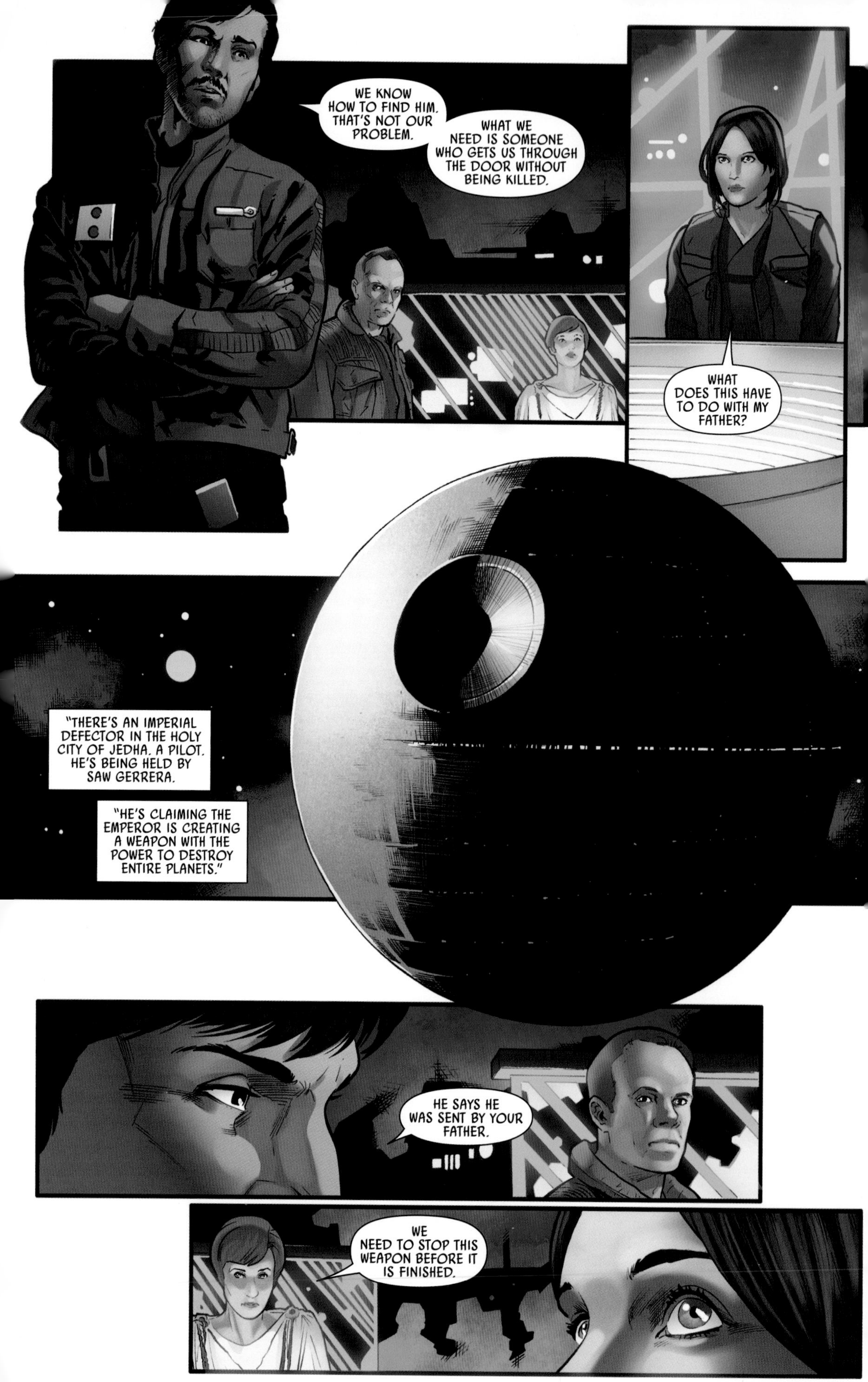
WE KNOW HOW TO FIND HIM. THAT'S NOT OUR PROBLEM.
WHAT WE NEED IS SOMEONE WHO GETS US THROUGH THE DOOR WITHOUT BEING KILLED.
WHAT DOES THIS HAVE TO DO WITH MY FATHER?
"THERE'S AN IMPERIAL DEFECTOR IN THE HOLY CITY OF JEDHA. A PILOT. HE'S BEING HELD BY SAW GERRERA.
"HE'S CLAIMING THE EMPEROR IS CREATING A WEAPON WITH THE POWER TO DESTROY ENTIRE PLANETS."
HE SAYS HE WAS SENT BY YOUR FATHER.
WE NEED TO STOP THIS WEAPON BEFORE IT IS FINISHED.

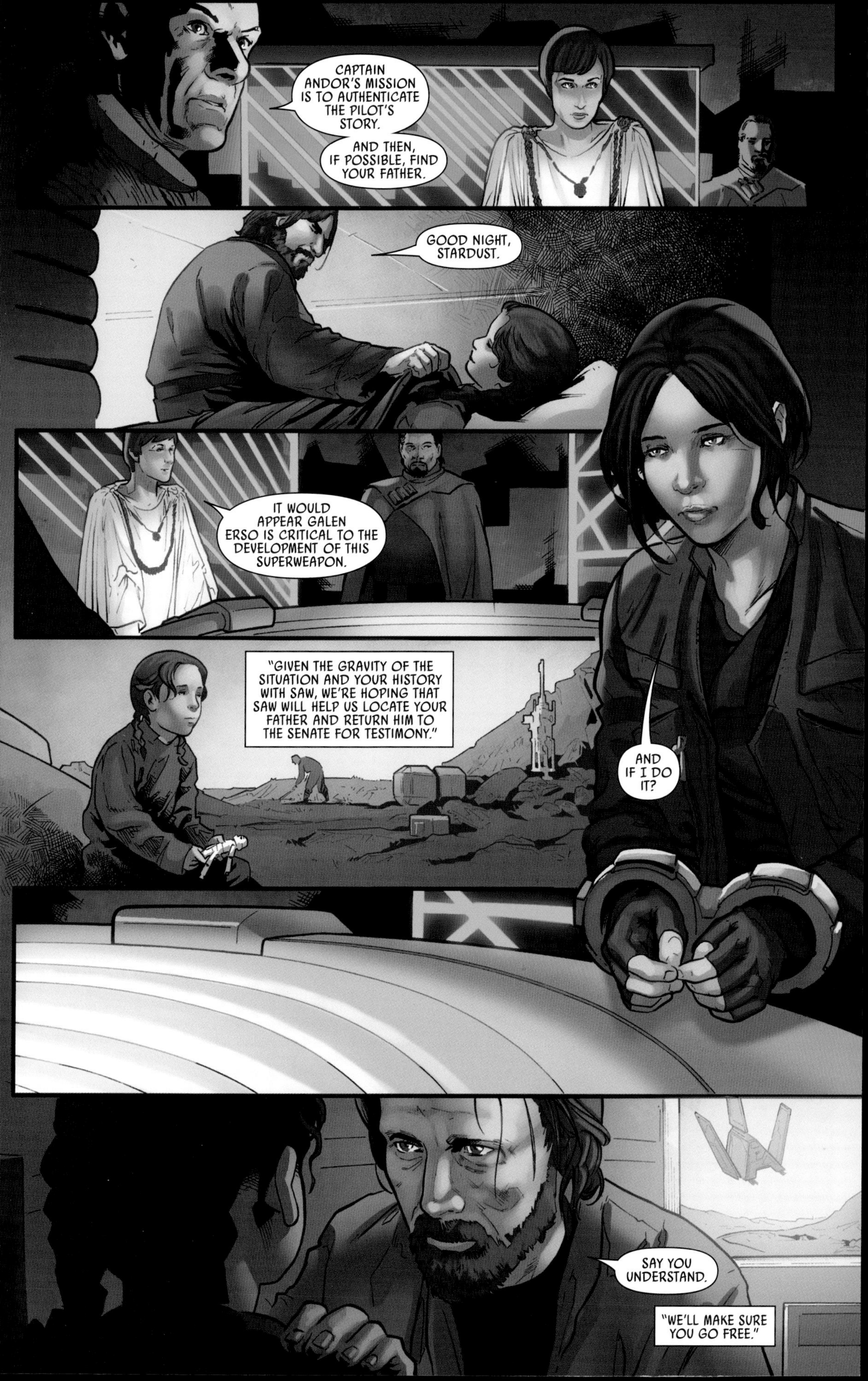
CAPTAIN ANDOR'S MISSION IS TO AUTHENTICATE THE PILOT'S STORY.
AND THEN, IF POSSIBLE, FIND YOUR FATHER.
GOOD NIGHT, STARDUST.
IT WOULD APPEAR GALEN ERSO IS CRITICAL TO THE DEVELOPMENT OF THIS SUPERWEAPON.
"GIVEN THE GRAVITY OF THE SITUATION AND YOUR HISTORY WITH SAW, WE'RE HOPING THAT SAW WILL HELP US LOCATE YOUR FATHER AND RETURN HIM TO THE SENATE FOR TESTIMONY."
AND IF I DO IT?
SAY YOU UNDERSTAND.
"WE'LL MAKE SURE YOU GO FREE."

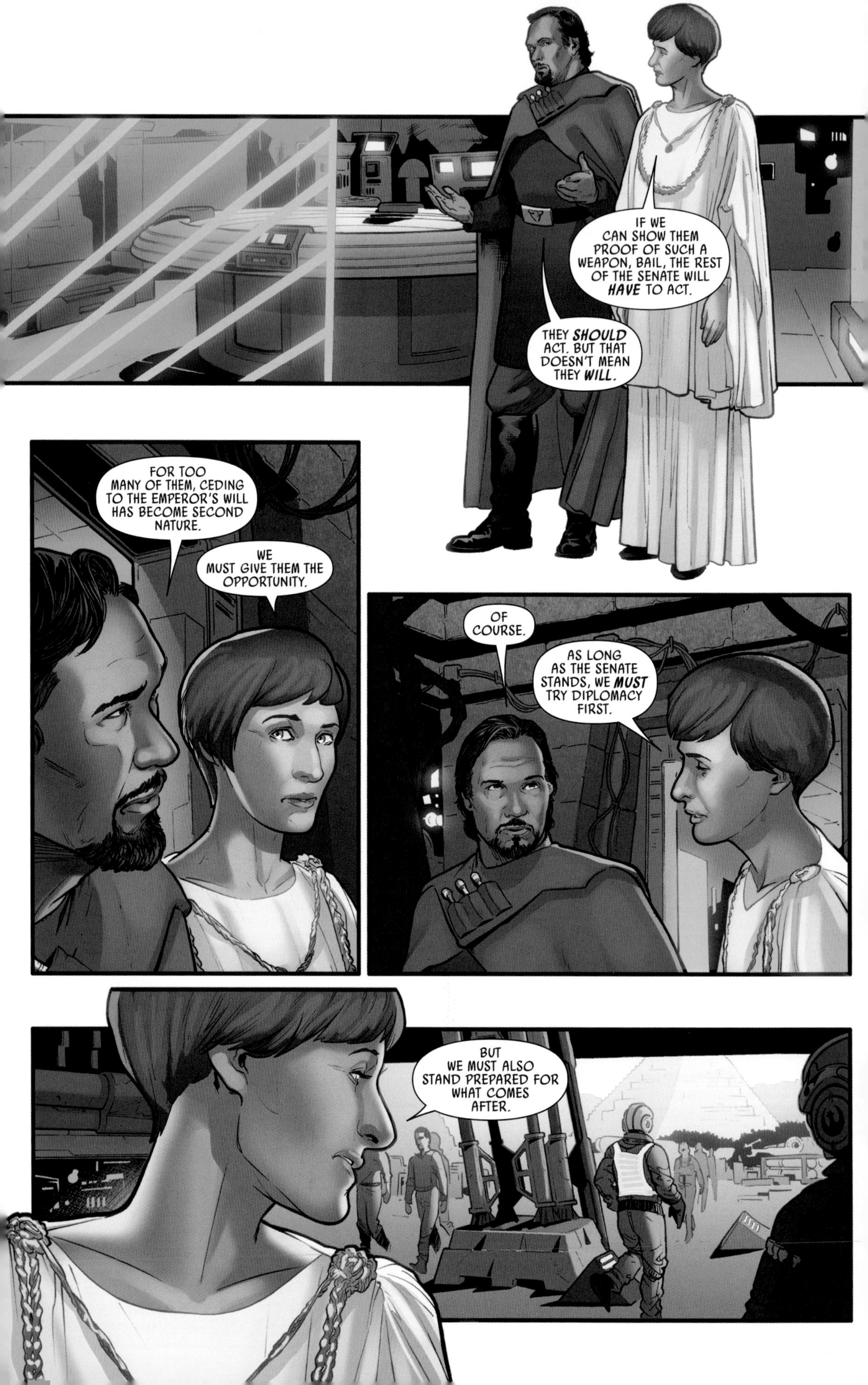
IF WE CAN SHOW THEM PROOF OF SUCH A WEAPON, BAIL, THE REST OF THE SENATE WILL *HAVE* TO ACT.
THEY *SHOULD* ACT. BUT THAT DOESN'T MEAN THEY *WILL*.
FOR TOO MANY OF THEM, CEDING TO THE EMPEROR'S WILL HAS BECOME SECOND NATURE.
WE MUST GIVE THEM THE OPPORTUNITY.
OF COURSE.
AS LONG AS THE SENATE STANDS, WE *MUST* TRY DIPLOMACY FIRST.
BUT WE MUST ALSO STAND PREPARED FOR WHAT COMES AFTER.

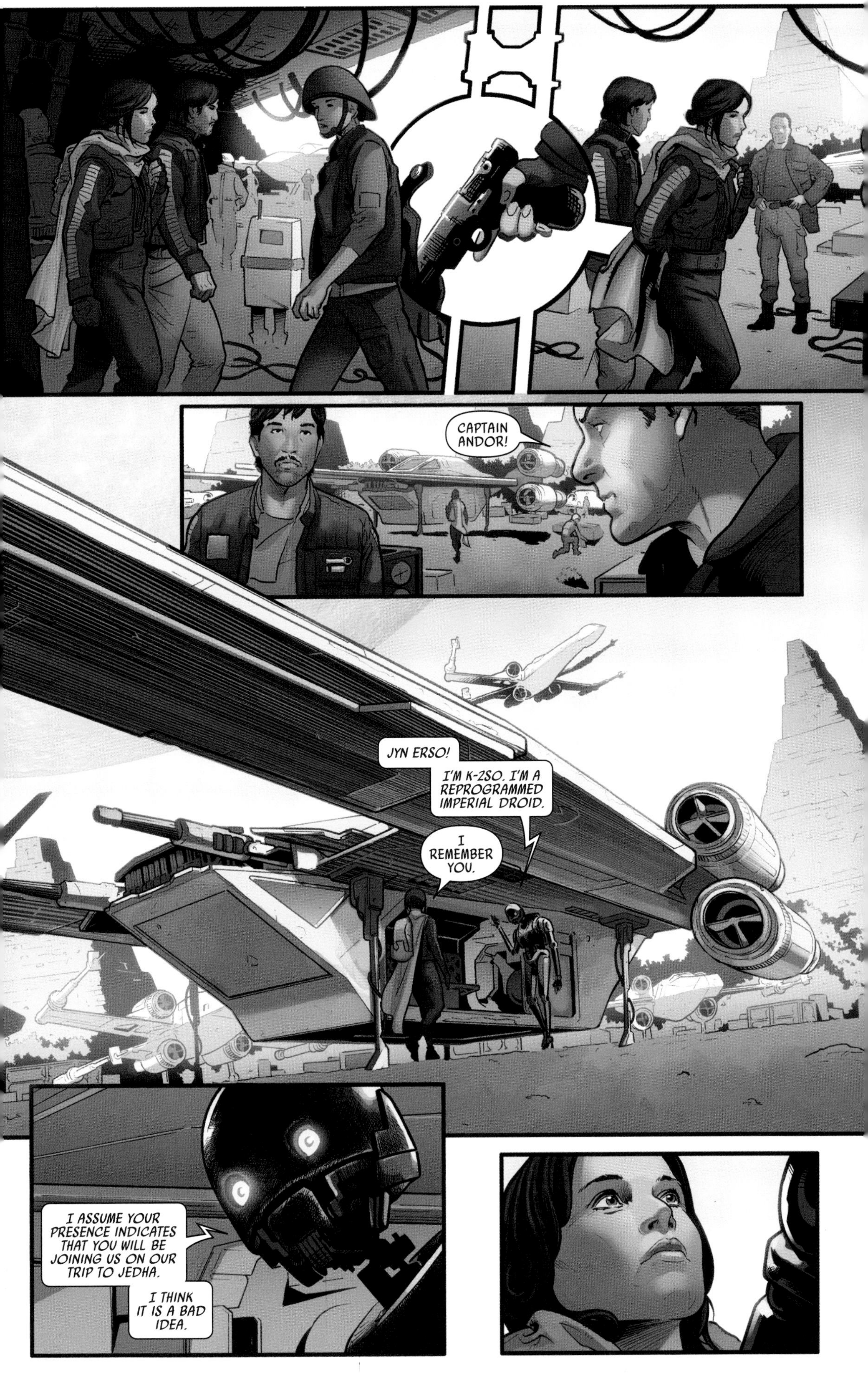
CAPTAIN ANDOR!
JYN ERSO!
I'M K-2SO. I'M A REPROGRAMMED IMPERIAL DROID.
I REMEMBER YOU.
I ASSUME YOUR PRESENCE INDICATES THAT YOU WILL BE JOINING US ON OUR TRIP TO JEDHA.
I THINK IT IS A BAD IDEA.

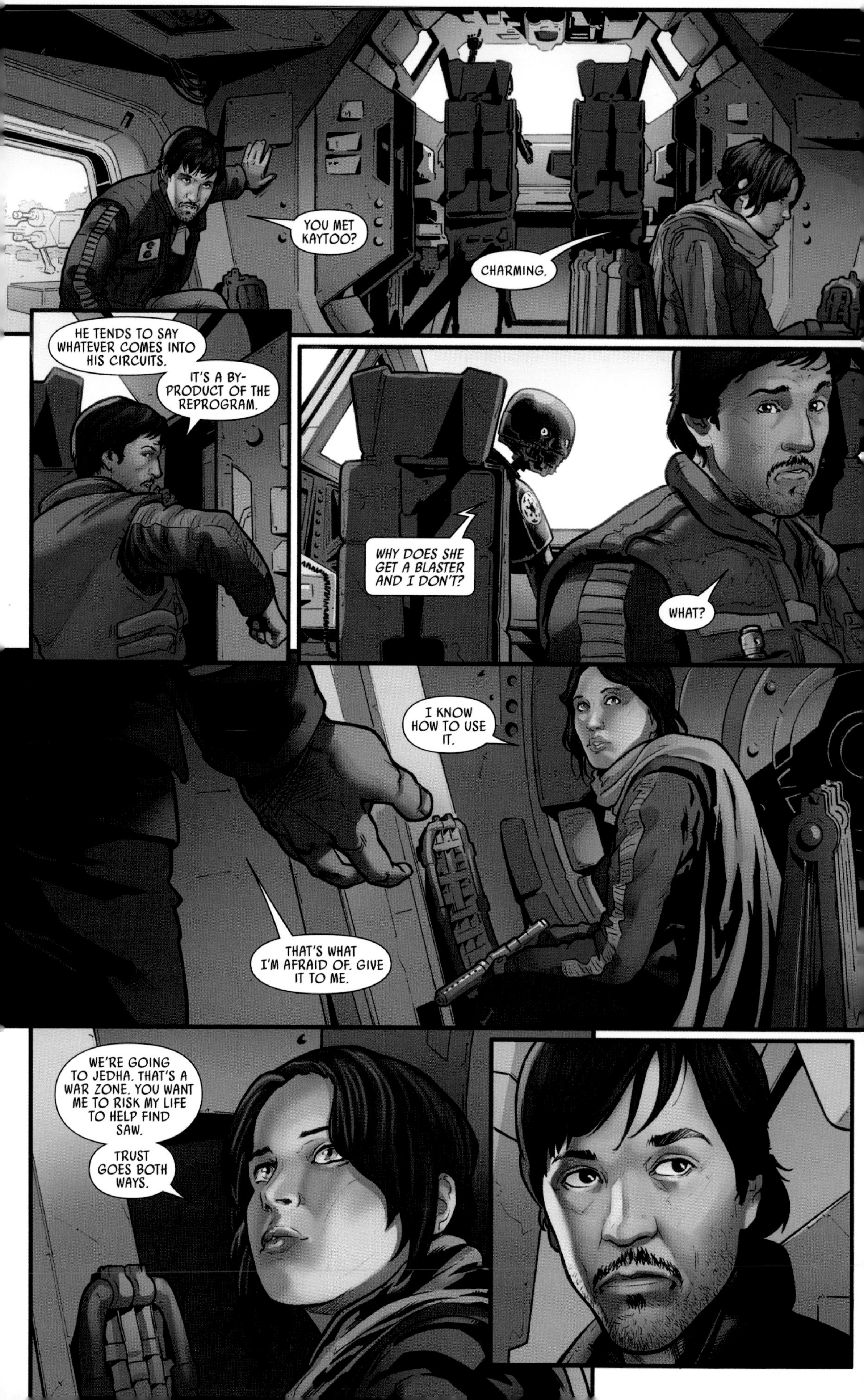
YOU MET KAYTOO?
CHARMING.
HE TENDS TO SAY WHATEVER COMES INTO HIS CIRCUITS.
IT'S A BY-PRODUCT OF THE REPROGRAM.
WHY DOES SHE GET A BLASTER AND I DON'T?
WHAT?
I KNOW HOW TO USE IT.
THAT'S WHAT I'M AFRAID OF. GIVE IT TO ME.
WE'RE GOING TO JEDHA. THAT'S A WAR ZONE. YOU WANT ME TO RISK MY LIFE TO HELP FIND SAW.
TRUST GOES BOTH WAYS.

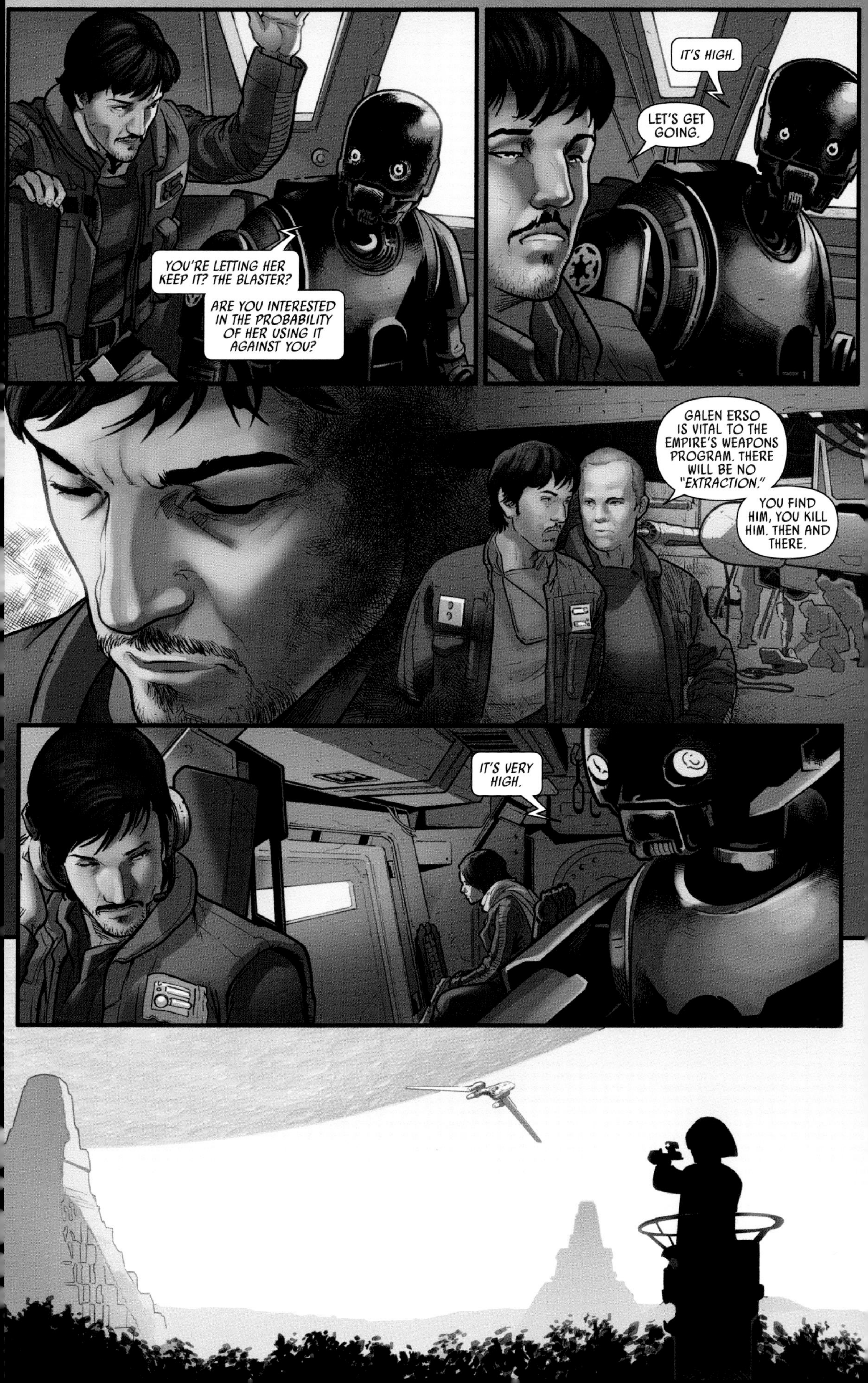
YOU'RE LETTING HER KEEP IT? THE BLASTER?
ARE YOU INTERESTED IN THE PROBABILITY OF HER USING IT AGAINST YOU?
IT'S HIGH.
LET'S GET GOING.
GALEN ERSO IS VITAL TO THE EMPIRE'S WEAPONS PROGRAM. THERE WILL BE NO "EXTRACTION."
YOU FIND HIM, YOU KILL HIM. THEN AND THERE.
IT'S VERY HIGH.

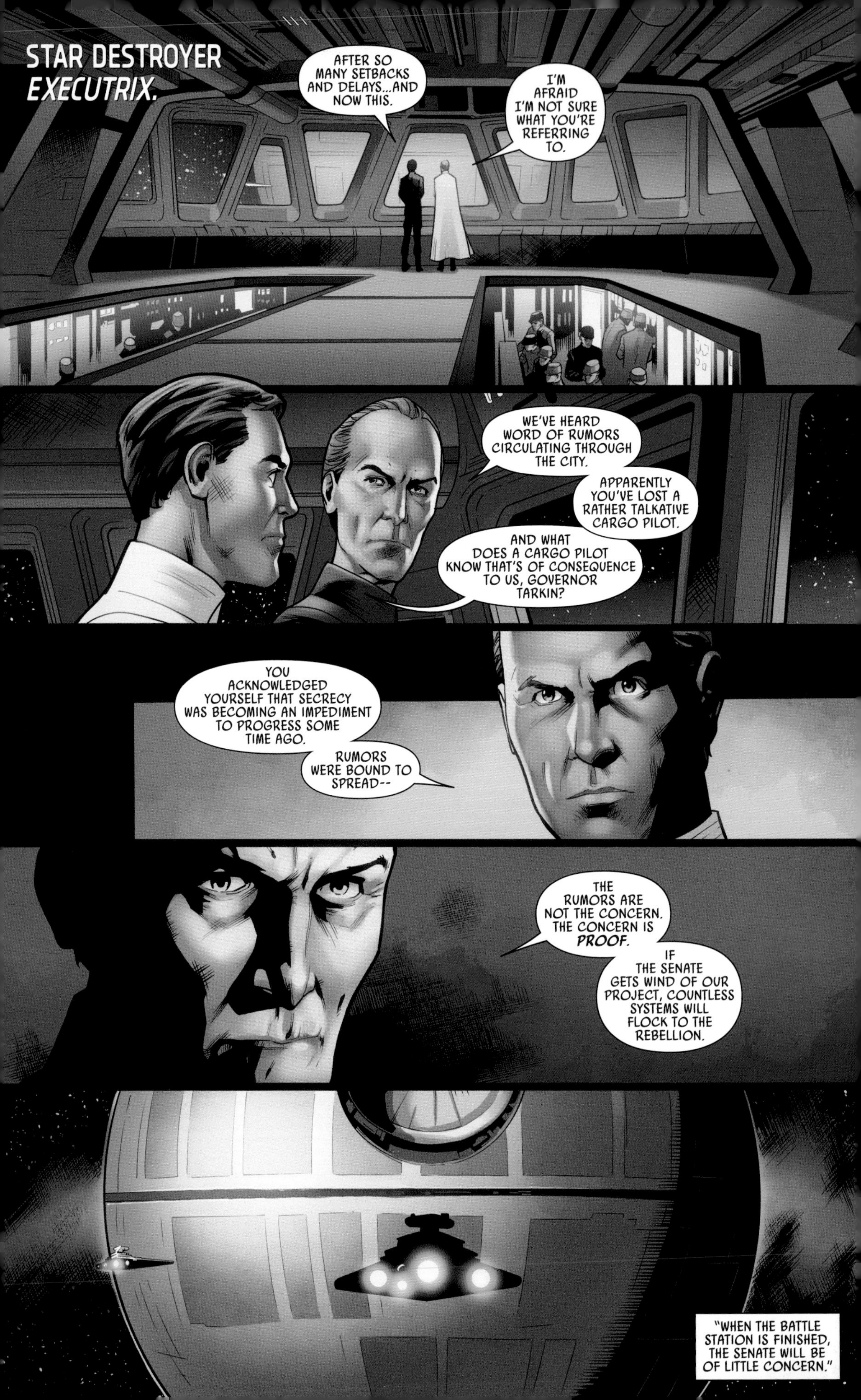
STAR DESTROYER *EXECUTRIX.*
AFTER SO MANY SETBACKS AND DELAYS...AND NOW THIS.
I'M AFRAID I'M NOT SURE WHAT YOU'RE REFERRING TO.
WE'VE HEARD WORD OF RUMORS CIRCULATING THROUGH THE CITY.
APPARENTLY YOU'VE LOST A RATHER TALKATIVE CARGO PILOT.
AND WHAT DOES A CARGO PILOT KNOW THAT'S OF CONSEQUENCE TO US, GOVERNOR TARKIN?
YOU ACKNOWLEDGED YOURSELF THAT SECRECY WAS BECOMING AN IMPEDIMENT TO PROGRESS SOME TIME AGO.
RUMORS WERE BOUND TO SPREAD--
THE RUMORS ARE NOT THE CONCERN. THE CONCERN IS ***PROOF.***
IF THE SENATE GETS WIND OF OUR PROJECT, COUNTLESS SYSTEMS WILL FLOCK TO THE REBELLION.
"WHEN THE BATTLE STATION IS FINISHED, THE SENATE WILL BE OF LITTLE CONCERN."

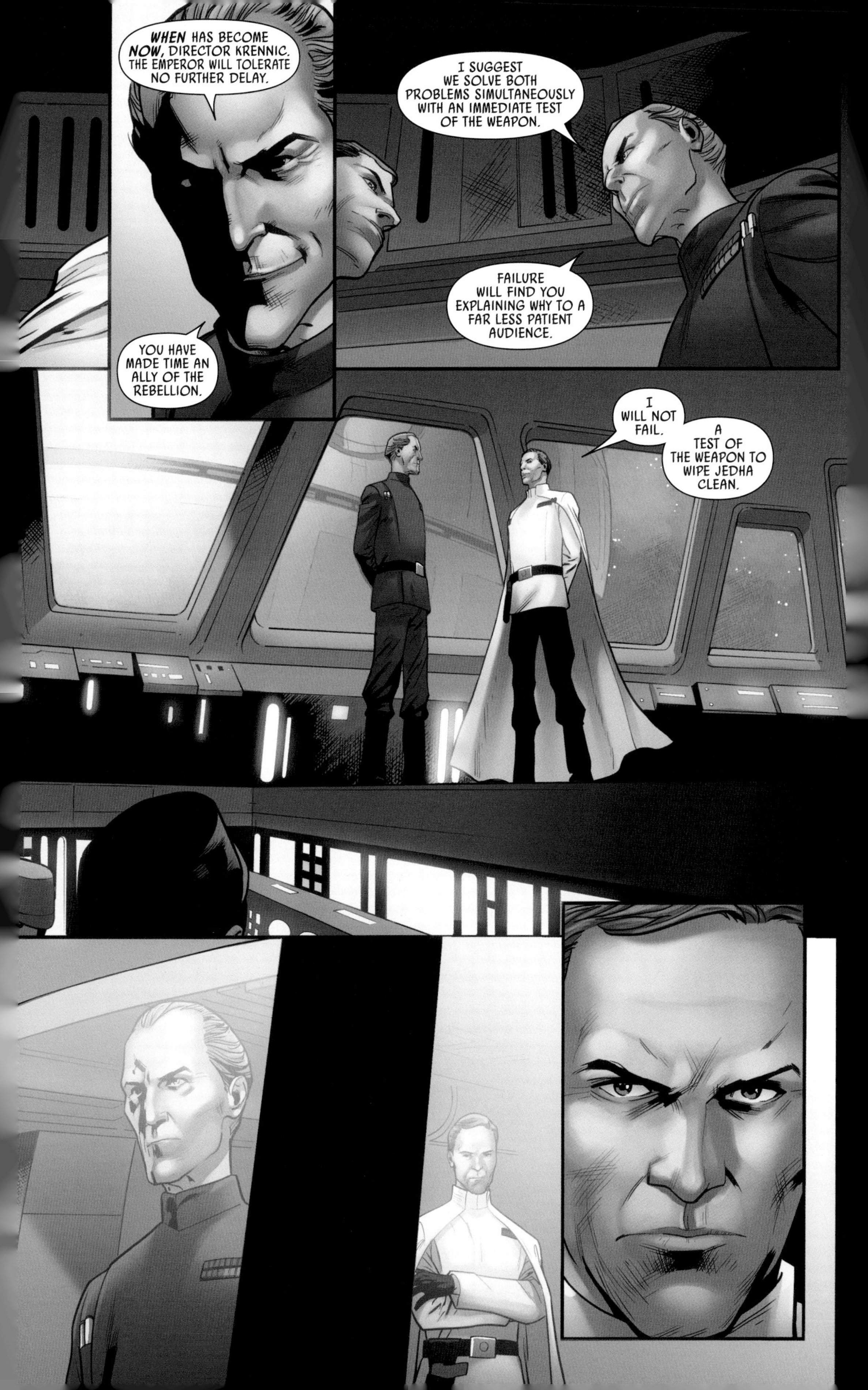
WHEN HAS BECOME NOW, DIRECTOR KRENNIC. THE EMPEROR WILL TOLERATE NO FURTHER DELAY.
YOU HAVE MADE TIME AN ALLY OF THE REBELLION.
I SUGGEST WE SOLVE BOTH PROBLEMS SIMULTANEOUSLY WITH AN IMMEDIATE TEST OF THE WEAPON.
FAILURE WILL FIND YOU EXPLAINING WHY TO A FAR LESS PATIENT AUDIENCE.
I WILL NOT FAIL.
A TEST OF THE WEAPON TO WIPE JEDHA CLEAN.

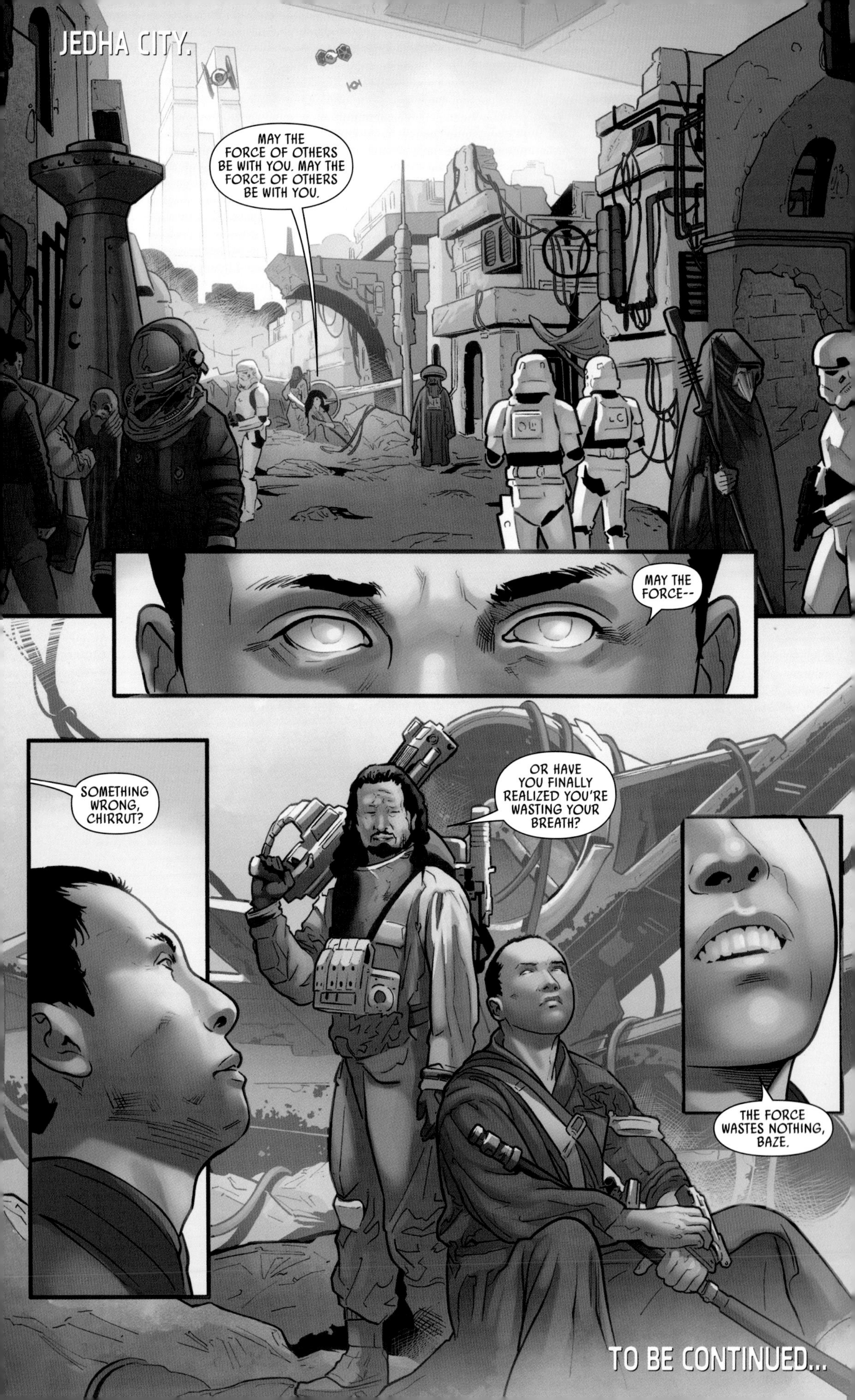
JEDHA CITY.
MAY THE FORCE OF OTHERS BE WITH YOU. MAY THE FORCE OF OTHERS BE WITH YOU.
MAY THE FORCE--
SOMETHING WRONG, CHIRRUT?
OR HAVE YOU FINALLY REALIZED YOU'RE WASTING YOUR BREATH?
THE FORCE WASTES NOTHING, BAZE.
TO BE CONTINUED...